W9-BAI-422

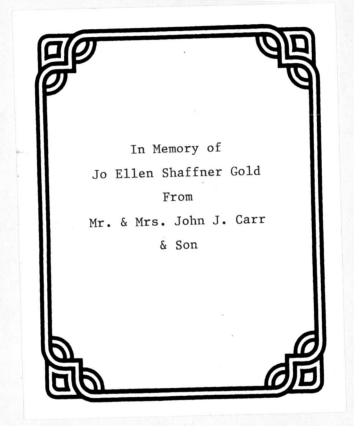

In Memory of
Jo Ellen Shaffner Gold
From
Mr. & Mrs. John J. Carr
& Son

Sea Horses

Sea Horses

JENNY HUGHES

BREAKAWAY BOOKS
HALCOTTSVILLE, NEW YORK
2013

MYS
J
HUG

ISBN: 978-1-62124-006-8
Library of Congress Control Number: 2013945594

Published by Breakaway Books
P.O. Box 24
Halcottsville, NY 12438
www.breakawaybooks.com

NOTE: For this edition, we have Americanized the spellings (for instance "color" instead of "colour"), but kept the original British vocabulary and usage. So, for anyone not familiar with some of these terms, here is a brief list with their American equivalents: rosettes= ribbons; downs=open fields with rolling hills; mate=friend; copse= a small group of trees; head collar=a horse's halter; numnah=saddle pad; school=riding ring; yard=stable area.

10 9 8 7 6 5 4 3 2 1

Chapter One

I didn't like where we lived. We've moved around a lot, Mum and I, but this town was easily the worst. It was big and ugly, with concrete buildings and hardly any trees or grass. My school was big too, and I spent half my day wandering along endless corridors trying to find whichever room I should be in. I could have asked, of course, should have made friends so I could just tag along with them, but I'm shy and find stuff like that difficult. Everyone seemed settled in their own group and although some of them smiled and said hi to the new girl, no one bothered with me much.

I'd had a few months of this so you can understand why I couldn't wait to get home, dump my books and my school clothes, pull on some jeans, and head off to meet Jade.

Jade was, and is, totally my Best Friend. She's beautiful, talented, clever, and sweet—everything you'd find pretty sickening in a BF—except that Jade is my wonderful pony. Mum made the decision to buy a horse for me when I was ten and she and my dad split up.

"I'm going to be the breadwinner from now on, Caitlin," she'd said, giving me one of her bear hugs. "And you know what that means. I have to be where the work is, so you'll have to put up with moving from town to town. Jade will be your constant: Wherever you go, she goes too."

That was nearly five years ago, and I'd grown to love the gorgeous bay pony more and more every single day. She had the temperament of a saint, taking each up-heaval happily in her stride, settling immediately in the new field or livery stable we found her, and, unlike me, enjoying herself and making friends with her new com-panions. I'd felt dead guilty when I unloaded her from the lorry and showed her where she was going to live this time. Bexworth Riding Center is on the edge of the sprawling town and is well run with big, airy box stalls for the horses and a fully equipped indoor arena, but it has hardly any land for grazing. The ponies are put into a field on a rotation, each having just a few hours a day; knowing how much Jade loved being outdoors, I absolutely hated the restriction. She, being Jade, was very good-tempered about the hours in her box, and I spent as much time as I could keeping her company. It was getting near the end of the school year and I was looking forward to the summer holidays when we'd be together practically all day, every day.

"Only two weeks to go." I pulled her velvet ears gently and she leaned against me. "Mum says we can go out into the country, ride anywhere we like. We'll take a picnic and you can eat all the grass you want."

She blew down her nose thoughtfully and nudged me agreeably.

"Maybe we'll spend a week somewhere—no, it'll only be a few days because she has to work." I prattled on to her like this all the time. "But we'll have a good holiday, I promise you."

As usual I spent longer than I meant chatting and grooming, and by the time we'd done forty-five minutes in the school, followed by another lengthy grooming session, I was late getting home.

"Caitlin, are you okay?" Mum sounded worried.

"Yeah, fine. Sorry, are you waiting to eat?" I hurried into the kitchen.

"No." She was all flushed and excited looking. "I thought we'd go out tonight, sort of a celebration. How's Jade?"

"Great. We did some flat work and tried a couple of jumps."

"Lovely." She started bustling round tidying up, something that doesn't come naturally to her.

"It was all right but we'd both rather be galloping across a moor or somewhere."

"Of course you would." She stopped trying to force a cereal box into an already full cupboard. "And—well, maybe you'll be doing that sooner than you think."

"Okay." I sighed. "Tell me what's happening. You're

changing jobs and we're moving again—right?"

"Well, um, not right away because so far this is just a one-off and if I mess up they won't want me again."

"You won't mess up," I said.

She's a brilliant photographer, specializing, or at least hoping to specialize, in pictures of wildlife.

"Thanks, sweetie, but this could be the big one!" She named a high-profile publication. "They're paying for me to spend a couple of weeks or so on the Galápagos Islands and if they like the results—"

"Wow!" I knew what this meant to her. "You've always wanted to go there!"

"I promised myself I'd go once you were grown up." She bit her lip. "But this is just too good an opportunity to miss so—"

"So?" I looked at her curiously. "What's the problem? Because there obviously is one."

"Well, for a start, it's the longest I've ever been away."

"No it's not. That bird-watching gig took nearly a month. Four weeks of getting up earlier than me for once."

"Oi, cheeky." She still wouldn't meet my eyes.

"Oh my God!" The realization hit me. "You mean you're going without me! You're going to leave me and Jade stuck here in Bexworth!"

"No, of course I'm not." She rubbed a hand violently through her hair.

"Don't do that, you look like a middle-aged punk." I couldn't believe she was going to abandon us.

Most of her work is done from a city office, wherever it happens to be at the time, and she flies or drives to a location, returning to the office where she develops and edits her photos. Sometimes when a "special," like the bird-watching contract, comes up, the three of us take off together and rent a holiday cottage or something, but she's never, ever taken on a project that takes her away on her own.

"Caitlin, honestly this is something major." Her hair was still sticking up in spikes. "If I get this right it means a long-term contract. We could settle somewhere really nice instead of moving from one crummy town to another."

10

"Somewhere nice?" I reached out and smoothed her hair. "Somewhere with land for Jade? Somewhere with proper riding?"

"Absolutely," she said fervently. "The company is international; I could work from home and do everything through the Internet instead of having to check into an office every day."

"Yeah, well, it sounds great and of course you've got to give it your best shot, but—" I paused. I left off my obvious question: *But what about me?*

"I know." She moved in for a hug. "You can't be left here, obviously, so I found some websites and thought you could choose before we go out tonight."

"Choose?"

"A holiday. I don't have to leave till school's finished so you can spend the time I'm away having a lovely holiday."

"On my own? I get to stay in a hotel or something on my own. Terrific." I did a double take. "And what about Jade? There's no way I'm leaving her—"

"Of course you're not." She dragged me off to her little study. "Where you go, she goes, I know that. So take a look at these websites, riding holidays where you take your own horse—there are centers up in the mountains, along riverbanks, the coast—or, hey look, there's a place that's right in the middle of a wild moor!"

I sat down in front of the computer and started scrolling. The moorland one was great and there was a place in a lush green valley where the riding looked terrific, but to me one place stood out.

"Beacon Lodge," I read aloud. "Acres of grazing, schooling facilities, clifftop rides, beach picnics, and a varied program of competition."

"Sounds good," Mum said. "But then they all do. What's special about that one?"

I pointed to a picture on the Beacon Lodge home page where a group of young riders were cantering through the spray on the edge of the ocean, while farther out two horses were swimming blissfully with their smiling owners.

"I've always wanted to swim in the sea with Jade." I closed my eyes at the thought. "She'd love it."

"Yeah? That's the one then. And you'll be doing competitions too. You said you wanted to enter more horse shows."

"Yeah I do." I was still transfixed by the photograph of the swimming horses, noticing the way the light glinted on their sleek, wet skin and turned the waves around them to silver.

"That *does* look brilliant," Mum said, looking over my shoulder. "So if I get you and Jade booked in there, you'll forgive me?"

"Don't be soft." I turned and grinned at her. "There's nothing to forgive."

"That's my girl. Come on, let's go out and grab a pizza."

I dived in the shower to remove any traces of horsiness. I always think smelling of Jade is a good thing, but not everyone agrees. The pizza place was buzzing and I felt a matching stir of excitement at the prospect of the holiday. I couldn't wait to tell my pony, of course, and left even earlier than usual to make my early-morning call at the stables. The yard was deserted, very clean and tidy; only a few horsey heads were looking out over their doors, blinking at the first pale rays of the sun. I walked quickly to

Jade's box and looked in. She was still asleep, stretched out on a nice deep bed, her breathing slow and rhythmic. As I slid back the bolt and stepped inside she woke, lifting her head to look at me.

"Hello, baby," I crooned. "I've got some news!"

She made her usual welcoming sound, gently blowing through her nose and nudging me happily as I curved my arms around her neck. When I first got her she'd always get to her feet as soon as I approached if she'd been lying down; it took months before she trusted me enough to let me sit alongside her. Now, though, she just loved to lie with me while I cuddled and petted her, nestling against me more like a cute puppy than 14.2 hh of well-muscled pony. I told her all about Mum's job opportunity and of course about the fabulous-looking Beacon Lodge.

"Acres of fields, you can live outdoors all the time—and the riding! Jade, it's going to be fantastic, we can improve our jumping, maybe try cross-country, and guess what?"

She pushed her nose firmly into me as if to say, "Go on, tell me."

"It's right by the beach! We can go swimming in the ocean together!"

Yeah, all right, maybe Jade didn't understand all the words, but she could tell from the tone of my voice that I was excited and happy so, being my Very Best Friend, she felt the same way too. I got her ready for her morning exercise, another forty-five minutes in the school. Although she put in a good session, she ended it with a series of exuberant little bucks that nearly sent me over her head.

"A few good gallops along the clifftop will soon settle your nonsense." I kissed her nose as I removed her bridle. "You've got too much excess energy, Jade. Wait till we can burn some of it up on this holiday of ours."

I was looking forward to the experience so much, the last two weeks of term really dragged. I knew we'd been lucky to get a vacancy at Beacon Lodge. Mum had managed to grab a last-minute cancellation and was busy making arrangements for a lorry to take me and my pony on the journey to the coast.

"I just hope you're going to enjoy this as much as you

think." She watched me indulgently as I bounced around my room working out what to pack. "And you don't seem at all bothered about missing me. I'm officially offended, Caitlin."

I stopped prancing about with a T-shirt on my head and gave her a quick hug. "It'll be weird not having you around but you'll be having a wonderful time too and I've got Jade, remember."

"It would be nice if you managed to make some human friends too." She was rummaging in my dirty clothes bin. "Any chance, d'you think?"

"Yeah maybe," I said cautiously. "We're bound to have a lot in common, aren't we, you know all being riders and horse lovers together."

"Mm, though I've never seen anyone quite as besotted with their pony as you are," Mum said darkly. "You don't even bother with boys! I'll put this sweater in the machine, shall I? It's your favorite."

"Yeah, thanks." I grinned at her. "Don't tell me you're trying to get me hooked up with someone! I can't stand the guys at school, they're a bunch of pimply morons."

"Charmingly put. Maybe you should consider what you say before sharing that kind of opinion with your fellow guests at Beacon Lodge."

"I'll try. How many others will there be? Did they tell you when you got the booking?"

"They take six and this time it's evenly matched, three fellas, three girls."

"Oh, I'll see if I can get married to one then," I said mockingly. "Only Jade will have to be bridesmaid, of course."

She responded by tipping the rest of the laundry bin over me. We spent a spirited ten minutes having a sock fight.

"I don't know about your horse," she panted as I pelted her with the hated school gear. "You could do with expending some of your own energy—I just hope swimming in that ocean is going to calm you down a bit!"

At last, though it felt like months rather than weeks, the great day arrived. Jade and I were leaving at eight o'clock in the morning, and I was up and ready to go before Mum even surfaced.

"Come on, lazy," I said, thumping on her bedroom door. "I know your flight's not till this afternoon but you've got to see me and Jade off soon."

She stumbled into the kitchen with bleary eyes and tousled hair and squeaked when she saw the time.

"It's practically the middle of the night! You don't go for three hours yet!"

"I have to give Jade her breakfast and get her and her stuff ready for the horsebox," I defended myself. "And you're taking my backpack with all my clothes and stuff, remember, so you've got to come with me."

"You go to the yard now and manicure your horse's hooves or whatever." She turned back to her room. "I'll join you at eight to say good-bye."

"You've got to say it properly," I yelled at her retreating back.

"Okay," she said, yawning. "Seven thirty then."

Honestly, I thought. *How she's going to get on if they want her to photograph something at dawn I just don't know!*

I made my usual fuss of Jade but instead of riding her

I gave her an hour in Bexworth's small paddock while I mucked out her stable and got all her tack and everything ready to take with us. She enjoyed stretching her legs in the field but trotted over to the gate immediately when I whistled for her. By the time the horsebox pulled into the yard I'd done everything and was glad to see Mum's little car following the lorry in. She rushed over with my rucksack and some sweets for me and Jade on the journey, and for one awful moment I thought she was going to cry.

"So—you're all packed too, I hope." I made my voice brisk and jolly. "Passport, tickets—oh, and don't forget your camera!"

"I think I've got everything." Her lower lip was still trembling a bit. "But it still feels unnatural to be going without you."

"It'll be great," I said firmly. "Think of all those exotic creatures you're going to get on film. Best photos ever seen, remember."

"I'll do my best." She managed a bright smile and a hug. "Make sure you and Jade have a good time."

"*No* problem." I clambered into the lorry's cab and

waved cheerfully. "Bye, Mum."

As we drove out of the yard I could see her in the wing mirror, still smiling bravely, and I waved till she was out of sight, then kept my head turned resolutely to the window so the driver wouldn't see the big, fat tear that was trickling down my face. He didn't mention it, not being so much tactful as taciturn. We drove the long miles to the coast without saying very much at all, and I found the breezy confidence I'd been displaying ebb slowly but surely away. What if Beacon Lodge was nowhere near as good as it claimed? What if the paddocks were horrible, the surrounding countryside ugly, the sea too rough to swim in? What if, I thought with rising panic, the people were nasty and instead of the smiling, happy faces of the riders I'd seen in the photo they were a miserable, bad-tempered bunch? What if—

"There it is." The driver spoke at last as he pointed ahead. "Beacon Lodge."

A long drive wound its way between neatly fenced fields of lush green grass. There were trees and flowers everywhere; in the distance, a lovely old house glowed in the early-afternoon sun. A lone rider mounted on a fine black Thoroughbred was waiting at the gate as we slowed down to make our approach.

"Hi." He leaned forward and smiled into my face. "You must be Caitlin. I'm Zak Meadows, son of the owners. Welcome to Beacon Lodge."

Chapter Two

Whenever I see someone riding I always, always look at the horse before I check out the rider. This one was a real stunner, the color of gleaming ebony with the fine head and classic lines of a Thoroughbred. I noted the strong curve of his neck and his kindly, dark eyes and knew from his superb muscle tone that in motion he'd really be something to see.

"Hello," I greeted his rider almost absently. "Yes, I'm Caitlin."

"Great." He sat back and I looked at him properly for the first time.

He was nineteen or twenty, I reckoned, tall and slim but well muscled, and he had the brightest blue eyes in the most handsome tanned face I'd ever seen.

"I'm just taking Jet out on a—sort of errand. We won't be long." His smile was nice too. "Drive straight into the yard and there'll be someone there to welcome you properly."

"Fine, thanks." I watched him turn Jet and move away, trotting on the springy turf track before flowing effortlessly into canter.

"Down here, is it?" The monosyllabic driver put the lorry into first gear.

"I guess so." I looked out the window with interest and was about to jump down and open a big double gate when it swung easily open and we drove at last into the Beacon Lodge yard. It was lovely, not too big, with a dozen or so stables clustered companionably round the paved center. A tall man, middle-aged and balding, but with features startlingly like Zak's, walked toward the lorry, a big smile on his face. I hopped out of the cab and held my hand out awkwardly. He shook it politely and we swapped names—his was Ed Meadows—then he asked if we'd had a good trip.

"Fine thanks, but can I get Jade out straightaway?"

"Of course." He and the driver unhooked the ramp and I led my beautiful pony down it, stroking her neck proudly.

"Very nice, Caitlin." Ed's voice was approving. "And not a drop of sweat on her either."

"She's a really good traveler." I still checked every inch, though, while Ed unloaded all our stuff from the lorry.

He offered the driver a drink but Mr. Silent shook his head and said he was going to park up and have a sleep in the cab before he set off back to Bexworth.

"Hiyah! Ooh I like your horse." A girl about my own age, with short dark hair, came moving quickly toward us, also beaming.

"Thanks. She's Jade and my name's Caitlin. Do you— um—work here too?"

"No, I'm Millie, a guest like you, only this is my second time at Beacon Lodge so I'll show you around if you like."

Ed grinned at her. "D'you know, I thought that was my job!"

"Oh, you're busy and Caitlin would rather get the low-down from someone like me."

He picked up my saddle and grooming kit and raised his eyebrows at me. "Let me stow this stuff in the tack room and I'll be with you."

"It's fine with me if Millie wants to do it," I said diffidently, feeling shy at the unaccustomed attention. "The main thing I want is to get Jade settled, and I'll probably take ages doing that."

"You're the last one to arrive and everyone else has chosen to turn their horses out, but you can stable her if you'd rather. Our fields are bigger than a lot of ponies are used to, so if you think she'll be difficult to catch—"

"No, she's always brilliant," I said swiftly.

"Millie will show you where then. We've checked that all the horses have their vaccinations and worming up to date—just like Jade—so off you go."

I'd taken all my pony's travel gear off and now she walked beside me, keeping level with my shoulder and looking around her with great interest.

"She's amazing." Millie seemed very relaxed and chatty. "My boy, Chas, was a complete lunatic when we unloaded him, all wild-eyed and panicky. I tried him in a stable first of all but Zak said put him in the field, he'll soon calm down, and he did."

"I met Zak just now." I waited while Millie unlatched another gate. "He was going somewhere on Jet, said he wouldn't be long."

"Yeah, well, I'll believe that when I see it," Millie said cryptically. "He's gone off to see Tasha, so he could be ages."

"Tasha?"

"His girlfriend." She gave a deep sigh. "Good looking, of course, but a total pain."

I didn't quite know how to respond to that so I said lamely, "Oh, right."

"You'd think, wouldn't you, that a gorgeous guy like Zak would have the most perfect girlfriend in the universe but—oh here we are. I'll get the gate again."

We'd arrived at the well-fenced perimeter of a huge field that stretched away to a line of trees in the distance. The grass looked good; there were two big, clean water troughs, and about eight horses grazed contentedly in a group away to our right.

"It's okay, I'll do it, thanks." I slid the latch and walked Jade through, getting her to stand politely as I shut it again.

I'd have liked to do our kiss-and-cuddle routine but knew I'd feel pretty self-conscious in front of a new acquaintance so took off her head collar straightaway and waited. She blew gently into my face, her velvet nose brushing my skin.

"Your holiday starts now, baby," I whispered. She gave me a last affectionate nudge before moving away.

"Chas dragged me nearly halfway across the field, couldn't wait to get out there." Millie was impressed.

"Jade always likes to say good-bye properly." I watched intently as my pony approached the other horses.

A rangy-looking chestnut raised his head and surveyed her, whinnying loudly.

"That's my Chas." Millie hopped onto the fence to watch. "Oh, and there's Fenton, he looks interested too."

The iron-gray Fenton was the first to reach Jade, standing in front of her and arching his neck. She tossed her head and they breathed in each other's smell as they stood quietly nose-to-nose. Now Chas wanted to join in so he pranced close and whinnied once more. Jade tossed her head again, sending her glossy black mane flying as she took off in a perfect extended canter. Chas plunged and cavorted, following eagerly, but it was the gray horse who joined her, cantering close alongside. The excitement spread to the other horses, and for a few minutes they galloped together across the open expanse of grass like a flock of birds reveling in the freedom of the skies. They looked absolutely stunning, and Jade, at their head, was a poem of movement, every turn, twist, and spin performed with style and grace. Soon they were slowing, the exuberant gallop becoming a canter, the wide, curving circles diminishing until the display petered out and the herd regrouped and settled. I saw Jade's nose drop to inspect the ground and then she too was happily grazing, all her concentration focused on cropping the short, sweet grass.

"Look at Fenton—he couldn't get much closer if he tried." Millie laughed and pointed to the dark gray head right next to Jade's pretty bay one.

"Who does Fenton belong to?" I asked, not taking my

eyes off my pony. "Is he one of the Beacon Lodge horses?"

"No, he's a guest horse, owner's called Tom and he was here last year too. Tom and Fenton are totally the best at Pony Club games, they can win at practically every game ever invented!"

"Oh." I felt a bit stupid telling her Jade and I had never even tried mounted games. "Are you and Chas good at that too?"

"We're not much good at anything if I'm honest," Millie said frankly. "Show jumping's our best bet unless it's against the clock."

"Why, what happens then?" I laughed at her expression.

"Sheer chaos." She pulled another face. "Chas gets so excited he forgets everything he's ever been taught and I lose all control so we end up hurtling round the ring like a runaway express train. I suppose you and Jade are brilliant at everything—you've sort of got that partnership look when you're together."

"Thanks." I hesitated, still feeling a bit shy. "We've done a bit of jumping but haven't entered many competitions so I don't know if we're any good."

"Oh, you'll soon find out. Zak organizes mini shows for us and Ed and Val are great teachers, so anything you're no good at they'll soon put right."

"Sounds good." I was feeling that buzz of excitement again, watching Jade settle in so beautifully and listening to Millie's entertaining, upbeat chatter. "The thing I'm really looking forward to doing is swimming in the sea. I reckon Jade is going to absolutely love it."

"Yeah? I thought that about Chas but it took nearly a week to get him in. He'd paddle but he wouldn't go any deeper."

"How did you persuade him in the end?"

"Zak did it. We go to the beach practically every day and he just persevered, encouraging us a bit farther each time, till suddenly there we were—swimming!"

"It looks amazing," I said with feeling. "I saw the picture on the website and—"

"Hey that's us—Chas and me!" She slid off the fence and struck a pose. "The two horses swimming in the picture are Chas and Fenton! Ed took the photo last year. I've got a copy on my bedroom wall—it's a terrific one of Zak, isn't it?"

"I didn't notice," I said honestly. "Was he one of the riders cantering through the surf?"

"You didn't—duh!" Millie stared at me in disbelief. "I reckon Zak is the reason most girls book to come here. Don't you think he's totally yummy?"

"He *is* cute," I agreed cautiously. "But he's definitely not why *I'm* here."

"You must be mad." She flopped to the grass and fanned herself dramatically with one hand. "Zak is so gorgeous, he's practically edible!"

"I'll take your word for it." I sat down next to her, still keeping a close eye on Jade. "He's way too old for me and anyway what about the beautiful girlfriend? Tasha, wasn't it? She must cramp everyone's style."

"She's all right, in fact she's quite a laugh sometimes, but she's high-maintenance—what's known as fiery. Which in my book means she's just plain argumentative."

"Not so good," I said, a bit nervously. "I don't like falling out with people so I think I'll try avoiding her. She doesn't actually work at Beacon Lodge, does she?"

"Well, she's at college, a drama student, wouldn't you know it, but that means she's on holiday now so she helps out here, mainly because Zak wants her around all the time."

"He's pretty keen then." I was getting bored with the subject. "So, while we're here, would you tell me the names of all the horses we can see, Millie?"

"Don't know them all, there are three other new guests besides you this time."

I sat up as Jade moved across the field and another bay lifted his head to look at her. "Who's that one?"

"Dunno. Your horse is *fine*, Caitlin, you don't need to worry. We could leave her now, you know."

"I'll just give it another five minutes or so." I looked at her apologetically. "Sorry, I'm just a bit—"

"Nuts about Jade?" She grinned at me. "Don't worry, I totally get it. Okay, I'll tell you the names I know—that palomino mare for instance—she's called Sabrina and she belongs to Tasha. The light gray gelding is Peter and he's Ed's, and the chubby roan is Val's horse, Rusty. I think I heard Zak say the piebald one is Lucas, and there's a girl who sounded a bit of a sap going on about her darling Teddy, so one of them is called that."

"Unless she was talking about a stuffed bear," I suggested, not very wittily.

Millie was kind enough to laugh. "Could be. Corinne, the girl's name is, and she's probably all right but I didn't take to her, you know how it is sometimes."

I felt flattered she seemed to have "taken" to me and said diffidently that we could go now if she liked.

"It's okay." She yawned and stretched out on the grass. "I'm not fussed till Zak's around. He usually takes us all across the cliffs for our first ride so we can look down at the beach and across the countryside. Last year he rode real close to me because Chas got so excited, Zak was worried my loopy horse would fall off the cliff."

"Real close?" I teased her. "Is that when you realized Zak was the perfect man?"

"Don't knock it, just you wait! I bet within twenty-four hours you'll be feeling like I do."

"No chance." I stood up and stretched, giving Jade one

last, careful scrutiny. "Maybe we should get back and meet up with the others."

"If you like," she said amiably, rolling over and getting to her feet. "They'll be in the garden. I'll show you."

The other four were, indeed, lolling around in a shady part of the pretty garden. They greeted us in friendly fashion.

"Sorry, I don't know all the names, only Tom from last year, but I'm Millie and this is Caitlin." My new friend helped herself to a cold drink from a tray.

"Hi, Caitlin." Tom, tall and fair-haired, handed me a glass. "Millie might have got to meet everyone properly if she hadn't shot off to find Zak as soon as she arrived. Anyway, this is Corinne, Andy, and Jacob."

We all murmured hello and how ya doing and I wondered if anyone else felt as shy and nervous as me.

"So Caitlin, are you new to this like me?" Corinne, who at fifteen and a half was a few months older than the rest of us, was pretty in a Barbie Doll kind of way.

"New?" I gaped a bit stupidly. "Um no, I've had Jade nearly five years and was riding about a year before that."

35

"No, I mean new to Beacon Lodge." She spoke s-l-o-w-l-y and clearly, obviously thinking I was pretty dumb. "I realize we're all experienced riders. Andy here is an ace cross-country exponent, for instance, and once he reaches sixteen he'll be top league."

"Oh really?" I said lamely. "I'm not top at anything, I'm afraid."

"Doesn't matter," Tom said easily. "Beacon Lodge is mainly for fun, though Val and Ed are great at teaching competitive riding if you want it."

"Caitlin just wants to swim in the ocean with her pony," Millie said through a mouthful of crisps.

"Yeah, I can't wait to do that as well." Jacob, the shortest of the three guys, moved in close. "Maybe Caitlin and me could go to the beach while you others are working on your jumping."

"We ride down to the ocean practically every day anyway," Tom said mildly. "It'll be more fun for Caitlin in a group."

"Yeah, I'd like that." I smiled at him gratefully, slightly freaked out by Jacob's over-keenness. "And anyway I want to improve my show jumping. Jade's brilliant and I don't want to hold her back."

"Jade's a pretty name," Corinne said brightly. "What color is she?"

"Bay," I said, then, feeling that was a bit abrupt, added, "A light bay with jet-black mane and tail."

"Oh, like my Teddy," she enthused. I tried hard not to look at Millie, who was grinning wickedly.

"How were all the horses when you checked?" Andy asked her. "Blaze settled down the minute I turned him out, couldn't believe it."

"Yeah, they were all great, had a bit of a run-around when Caitlin put Jade in the field but we stayed and watched for ages—"

"And they were all fine," I put in hastily, not wanting her to tell them how obsessively I'd watched my pony.

I was surprised how comfortable it was chatting to them all, though. I've never found it easy being part of a group, but the fact the conversation was all about horses made it more natural than usual for me to join in. We chilled out for another half an hour or so and I felt myself starting to relax and enjoy their company, even finding the very girlie Corinne and slightly intense Jacob were no problem. By the time Ed came over to see us there was a lot of laughing going on and his broad smile became even wider.

"You seem a happy lot," he commented. "How about a guided tour? Or is that too serious?"

"A tour would be good." Jacob jumped up immediately, but Millie waved a lazy hand.

"Nah. I already know this place like the back of my hand."

"Okay." Ed winked at us. "The rest of you come and meet Zak, he'll be the one showing you around."

"Oh, all right then." Millie tried unsuccessfully to look cool. "I might as well join in."

She somehow managed to sidle around Corinne and get right next to Zak as he took us round the fabulous grounds, showing us the impressive school, the beautiful field containing a scary cross-country course, and some of the outbuildings and trails.

"You've all been shown your rooms and the rest of the

house, right?" Zak's teeth flashed white in the good-looking face.

"Er, no I haven't." I realized I didn't even know where my backpack was. "I just settled Jade in the field and then hung out in the garden."

"Sorry, Caitlin." He moved quickly to my side. "Your bag will have been taken to your room, I'll show you where."

As we started walking up the stairs he stopped and took something from the hall table. "I'd better put this back in the office upstairs where it belongs. It's my dad's favorite paperweight—there's a real sea horse inside. Look."

I glanced briefly at the ornament, more interested in looking around me. The house was nice, cool and airy, and to my delight my bedroom window had a view of the paddock.

"Fantastic!" I leaned out blissfully. "I can see Jade first thing in the morning. There she is—look."

Zak craned his neck to see, squashed up so close beside me in the window that I could smell the clean, masculine tang of his skin.

"She's terrific." His brilliant blue eyes smiled into mine. "I can't wait to see you two together."

It must have been the excitement of beginning this holiday, I reasoned later, that made my insides perform a sudden, ecstatic lurch. I mean, what else could possibly have made me feel an emotion so strong, glorious, and completely unexpected?

Chapter Three

I didn't have any time to think about it; within seconds Zak had moved away and was leaving the room.

"I'm taking a short ride across the cliffs in half an hour." He turned at the door. "So if you want to come along, get your riding gear unpacked."

"Oh yes, please." I sounded slightly breathless even to me. "Um, see you in the yard then."

"Great." He gave one more teeth-flashing grin and disappeared.

Feeling distinctly light-headed I undid my backpack, got into my breeches, and put all my other stuff away in cupboards and drawers. Then I replaited my long hair, checked my appearance in the mirror (twice), and went downstairs carrying boots and hat. Tom was in the boot room and gave what I thought was a sarcastic wolf whistle when I walked in. I ignored him and, hearing Millie's voice outside, backed out again.

"Hi Caitlin." She grinned at me cheerfully. "You look good. I wish I had legs up to my armpits like that!"

"Funn*ee*," I said, tweaking her spiky brown fringe. "I thought somehow that you'd be on this ride, seeing that Zak's taking us out."

"You bet." She rolled her eyes and pretended to swoon. "With a bit of luck Chas will play up again and Zak will have to rescue me."

"You might get *really* lucky and it could even be me doing the rescuing." A grinning Andy nipped past us, followed by Jacob.

"Where's Corinne?" I asked as we all tugged our boots on.

"She's having a lie-down, tired out from the journey here." Tom was waiting by the door. "Come *on*, you lot."

We walked out together to the paddock, where the others started plodding their way over to the group of grazing horses. I stayed near the gate and gave one long, low whistle, watching with pleasure as Jade's head came up immediately. I whistled again and she began moving toward me, her trot quickly becoming a canter.

"Look at that." Millie stopped and stared. "Caitlin's horse can't wait to be with her!"

"Oh fantastic, she's bringing mine too!" Tom cheered as the iron-gray Fenton followed my pony, breaking eagerly into a fast trot to try and keep up with her.

Soon he too was cantering, and when Jade slowed and stopped in front of me Fenton slithered to an ungainly halt as well.

"Thanks, mate, you just saved me a walk." Tom slipped a rope round his horse's neck. "Lucky for me you've got good taste in women!"

"He's definitely fallen for my girl, hasn't he?" I gave Jade a welcoming cuddle and turned toward the gate. "He's been following her around ever since she arrived."

"I hope she's happy with that." For a moment Tom's gray eyes were serious, but then they widened. "Jade's just walking beside you—no head collar, nothing!"

"I don't really need one for her." I unlatched the gate and walked through, my pony at my side.

She turned neatly to wait while Tom and Fenton came through and then nudged the gate shut as I'd taught her.

"Phew!" Tom was really impressed. "Does she put her own saddle and bridle on as well?"

"Not so far, but I'm working on it." I grinned and we walked up to the yard, laughing and joking.

By the time the other three joined us with their horses we'd brushed, polished, and picked out feet and were waiting with saddles ready, showing off. Zak rode in on the gleaming Jet and I heard a wistful intake of breath from Millie when she saw him.

"Okay?" He grinned at us. "I think we'll have Caitlin and Jade next to me, followed by Jacob on Lucas, then Andy with Blaze. You two old-timers can bring up the rear, Millie, seeing as you know your way around so well."

I saw Millie's face fall and gave her an apologetic smile before moving Jade to ride alongside the black Thoroughbred. Zak opened the main gate with a remote control, and we moved off along the drive where long shadows fell across the grass from the late-afternoon sun. It was still warm, and a gentle breeze lifted the horses' manes a little as we turned left to follow a grassy track. This wound its way through a small copse, then climbed fairly sharply up the cliff side, the turf beneath us still short and springy, perfect for riding. Once the horses were warmed up Zak, sitting lightly in the saddle with the wonderfully arrogant ease of the born rider, moved Jet from trot into working canter. Jade, enjoying herself as usual, tried to plunge with him but I held her until I was ready, giving the smallest of touches to produce her free striding pace. Taking her up to join the black horse, I kept her in line with his handsome head, loving the exhilarating feeling of speed and tasting the first salty tang of sea breeze. We cantered the long length of the slope, and I could feel Jade buzzing with excitement as she too breathed in the exotic new flavor of the coastal air.

And then we were there—as the ground beneath us leveled, the ocean was stretched before us, the silver tinsel of every ripple turned to gold as the sun began its descent. The air was filled with the evocative sound of seagulls crying and the glorious crash of waves breaking on the rocks below. Zak reined his horse in and we sat taking in the spectacular sweep of the bay, its rocky, smoke-colored cliffs towering above the pale stretch of sand. Millie, her mind obviously not on the breathtaking scenery, walked Chas over to join us.

"Nice, eh?" She grinned at me meaningfully, nodding surreptitiously toward Zak. "The view I mean."

"It's—it's stunning," I said honestly.

"Look, Caitlin." Zak leaned forward. "Over there, a fishing boat coming home."

I tried to focus and he bent nearer, pointing in the right direction. "There, see?"

We were almost as close as we'd been in the window. I positively *felt* Millie bristle.

"Got it!" I moved quickly away, leaving her and Chas next to him.

Slightly shaken, I suppose I wasn't concentrating, and when a particularly vocal seagull swooped suddenly, making Jade spook, I just wasn't ready. Jade, used to the instant reaction of my calming hand, and fired up with the excitement of this wonderful new landscape, shied naughtily, throwing me off balance. The reins slid from my fingers, I lost both stirrups, and suddenly she was plunging forward completely out of control. I pulled myself together at once and would have regained my grip, my seat, and my poise—but Zak was quicker, racing alongside to grab the reins and bring us to a halt, only a few feet, I have to admit, from the edge of the towering cliff.

"Sorry!" I gasped.

He smiled directly into my eyes. "It's okay, don't worry."

My hair had come loose from its plait and flowed in a dark mass round my shoulders. I knew my eyes were huge as I stared, mesmerized, back at him. Convinced I looked like some kind of startled Bambi, I dropped my gaze and turned away, feeling bewildered and confused.

"You all right, Caitlin?" Tom's kind face was concerned.

"Yes thanks. My own stupid fault—I wasn't concentrating."

We moved on, keeping well away from the cliff edge and at a sedate walking pace. I was furious with myself and tried to stay at the back out of everyone's way, but Zak insisted I stay next to him.

He probably thinks I'm a nervous little novice rider incapable of keeping her pony under control, I told myself bitterly. *And now I've spoiled the first ride out for everyone else as well!*

I beat myself up about it for the whole time we were out, not even cheering up when Zak pointed down to the beautiful beach we'd be swimming from.

"A bit of work in the morning—we thought Pony Club games would be a good icebreaker—then down there tomorrow afternoon. Your first-ever swimming lesson with Jade. That'll be good, won't it, Caitlin?"

I grunted a yes but wouldn't look at him, feeling more and more gauche and stupid with every minute. For the first time ever I couldn't wait to finish a ride, and I got Jade back into the paddock in record time. There was a choice of games or a film to watch after we'd eaten but I just couldn't lift myself out of the black mood and took off upstairs on my own. I woke really early and lay in bed for a few minutes, listening to the birdsong and watching the room gradually lighten as the sun came up. I felt better, the inexplicable bad temper had left me, and though I was ashamed of myself I was also sure I could put the silly incident behind me and move on.

The first thing I did was to open the curtains and look out at the paddock, my heart lifting even further when I saw Jade contentedly grazing. Her new friend Fenton was close beside her again and I thought, not for the first time, how much better at getting on with life she was than me. I dressed and left the house quietly, entering the field and spending over an hour just being with my pony. After a while she lay on the grass beside me, closing her eyes blissfully as I stroked and petted her. I told her what a fool I thought I'd made of myself the day before, going on and on about it till she fell asleep, snoring gently with her head in my lap.

"You're making too big a deal of it, you know." Tom's approach had been so quiet I hadn't heard him behind me. "It was nothing, no one else was bothered—well, that's not exactly true, I guess."

"Oh?" I looked at him, still feeling embarrassed. "Zak,

I suppose? He must think I'm a totally inefficient moron."

"Shouldn't think so. Zak's seen a million guest riders and I'd put money on you being a lot better than most."

"Yeah?" I found I really, *really* wanted Zak to approve of me. "Who's mad about me messing up then?"

"Millie. She thinks you set up your little adventure so you could bat your big brown eyes and get all the attention from her beloved Zak."

"No way!" I couldn't believe it. "As if I'd deliberately make myself look a complete cretin!"

"You miss the point." He didn't look at me. "She thinks you did it to make Zak notice you."

"Oh my God!" I groaned. "It's *Millie* who's totally hipped on him, not me. And if I wanted someone to notice me I'd find a better way of doing it than making a complete fool of myself. And as for putting Jade in danger like that—" Words failed me.

I saw Tom's shoulders relax. "Just tell her that then, and she'll soon calm down. She's a nice kid, bit of a flake sometimes, especially where Lover Boy's concerned, but she's mostly all right."

I hesitated. "From what you just said I take it you're not that impressed with Zak yourself?"

"Don't mind me, I'm just jealous—the guy has every female within miles swooning at him so the rest of us are bound to feel a bit resentful. Zak's okay, really."

"I'll sort it out with Millie," I promised. "I'm sorry I didn't handle it very well yesterday. I don't know what was the matter with me."

"Maybe you were jet-lagged like Corinne," he said lightly, leaning over to pat the still-sleeping Jade.

She opened one eye and saw him, getting immediately to her feet.

"Sorry." Tom smiled at me ruefully. "Now I've gone and spoiled your cuddle."

"We'll have plenty more." I stroked my pony with one hand and slid the other round Fenton who, as usual, was very close by. "Hello, you."

The gray pony snorted amiably and nuzzled Jade's neck.

"He's got it bad." Again Tom didn't look at me. "I just hope she feels the same way."

"Do we bring them into the yard yet?" I asked. "Or is it still too early?"

He looked at his watch. "Yeah, a bit. We should go and have breakfast first, I think."

It was a cheerful, impromptu meal with all six of us helping ourselves from a selection of cereals, toast, and fruit while Val cooked eggs and stuff in the kitchen. Corinne, looked refreshed and pretty glamorous with full makeup and immaculate hair, was nibbling at some toast while Andy and Jacob sat beside her wolfing down king-sized omelets. Millie was there too, piling up a dish with fresh apricots and bananas. She saw me come in and her expression changed immediately.

"Hi." I walked toward her. "Can I join you?"

She tossed her head in best theatrical fashion and turned up her nose. "No thanks."

"Oh come on, Millie." I lowered my voice. "I'm really sorry I hacked you off yesterday but it was an accident, I swear. I'm not after Zak, not at all, honestly."

"Yeah right." She turned her back and went over to the window, as far away as she could.

I followed. "Jade does spook occasionally, she's not perfect and she can be a wicked mare sometimes. I wasn't concentrating—if I had been, I'd have stopped her okay. Zak was just quicker, that's all."

"Don't give me that." She was really upset. "I saw the way you looked at him, and I'd already told you how to keep him real close. You really went for it, didn't you, shaking your hair all loose and giving him the wide-eyed 'oh Zak you're my hero' treatment."

"You've got it all wrong." I pushed away the memory of the tremor Zak's proximity had sent surging through my body. "I was shook up, that's all, and let's face it I must have looked stupid, gaping at him like a fish."

"You weren't flirting?" She looked at me warily. "All that hair tossing and stuff?"

"The elastic band on my plait broke," I said impatiently. "And I might not know much about flirting but I reckon acting like a total fool isn't the one of the best ways to do it!"

"You were dead quiet afterward." Poor Millie still wasn't convinced. "Zak was concerned, he kept coming over and trying to talk you round."

"Just doing his job," I said wearily. "Making sure the customers are happy, that's all."

"Yeah." She gave a small smile. "And you don't think he's gorgeous?"

"He's all right," I said cagily. "But he's like *years* older than me and he's got a girlfriend so he's not even in the equation."

"That doesn't stop me liking him." Then she brightened suddenly. "But hey, I reckon he's fallen out with Tasha! She didn't come round last night and he didn't go over there."

"Maybe he's dumped her." I wanted Millie to be happy again.

"Yeah, about time too!" The smile was back in place. "So, you having any breakfast or what?"

I laughed and went to get some. We sat with Tom, soon recapturing the easy familiarity of the previous day.

"Right." Tom pushed away his plate and stood up. "Let's go and bring in those horses and get them ready for a games contest!"

To my surprise I wasn't that nervous when, warmed up and ready, we rode into the small field Zak had gotten ready for the morning session. All the other riders had done at least *some* Pony Club games so I'd expected to feel awkward and novicey, but they were all so laid-back about my lack of experience it made me relax too. He started off with a demonstration of techniques—stuff I'd seen before from the sideline at shows but never really concentrated on. Zak asked me and Jade to stand alongside him so he could explain exactly what was going on. Millie shot me a suspicious look as I moved across to join him but I pulled a clown face at her and mouthed, *No way—he's all yours, remember!* Zak was really good at describing the games the others showed me, breaking down each movement so I'd understand its usage.

"Watch Tom now, Caitlin." We were several feet apart, intently studying the action. "It's always the first team to finish who wins, so to save precious seconds, Tom will vault onto Fenton's back while the horse is moving—watch the stages. First he runs alongside with left hand holding the reins on top of Fenton's neck, right hand grasping the saddle on the far side. Then he pushes off with both feet, springing upward with weight supported on his right arm. A smooth swing of the right leg and he's in the saddle, shortening reins, settling and gaining control all before his pony's completed two strides."

"I can do that!" I said excitedly. "I ride Jade barebacked and that's exactly how I—what's he doing now?"

"It's called a pyramid race, still fast and furious but the horse must stand perfectly still to allow each rider to stack up the pyramid—whoops, Millie's let Chas rush past and the whole thing's toppled over!"

I laughed with him, turning my head to look into his face, and as I did so Tom called out, "Look, there's Tasha—she's coming over!"

Zak's eyes swung straight to the approaching rider and I clearly saw the look of adoration in their brilliant blue depths. There was absolutely no doubt about the way he felt about his girlfriend. Unfortunately for me, I was also sure about the emotion that was coursing through my own being. For the first time in my life I was jealous, with an intensity that almost startled me into blurting out exactly how I felt.

Chapter Four

Luckily, I managed to keep my mouth clamped shut and watched silently as Zak rode his horse across the field to meet Tasha. He leaned forward and kissed her mouth lightly, and I saw her smile. She was about nineteen and beautiful, of course, slim but curvy, and the dark red hair pulled casually back from her delicate face rippled almost to her waist. Andy and Jacob were gawping at her in delight, tongues practically hanging out. Even Tom, who'd seen her before, looked mildly stunned.

"Hiyah." She brought her pretty palomino mare over to join us. "I'm Tasha—I promise I'll learn all your names as we go along."

"You already know mine," Millie said chirpily. "And

Tom. We were here last year, remember? We're doing Pony Club games today only Caitlin hasn't done it before."

"Oh right." Tasha had a great smile, and I tried not to notice the besotted way Zak was looking at her.

I thought it was just as well I was about to learn a whole batch of the new techniques I was going to need for competition games: It would give me a chance to pull myself together. I'd never had a crush on anyone before, but I had to recognize I had a *gigantic* one now. The breathless, swoony feeling I'd experienced twice the day before had been nothing to do with the excitement of starting a holiday or the fact that Jade had spooked out on the ride. It was being close to Zak Meadows that had done it, and the illogical, spiteful surge of jealousy had been directed at his girlfriend simply because she *was* his girlfriend! Before I could analyze the situation into a horrible muddle, I had to get on with the job in hand, which was riding a by now very hyped-up and excited Jade in our first-ever Pony Club game.

"A simple one to start with," Zak said. "It's called Musical Mats."

The concept certainly wasn't rocket science. We all cantered in a circle round bits of old sacking laid out on the
ground while music played. Tasha was in charge of a radio,
and when she switched it off we had to dismount and,
leading our ponies, get to one of the sack "mats" and stand
on it. Very straightforward, I thought as I put Jade into
canter behind Tom and Fenton. We rode two complete
circuits and the music stopped; I slid off and started jog-
ging toward the nearest mat—only to see Tom step
smartly onto it.

"Come on, Jade." Running faster, I headed off for the
next nearest, nearly reaching it before Corinne, who, pant-
ing slightly, jumped onto the middle of it. I looked round
wildly—everyone else was also standing on a mat, smugly
holding their ponies' reins. Sprinting now, I hurtled round
the circle to the last remaining sack—but just as I placed
a foot on it, Jade, obviously not understanding the game
at all, kept going, taking me with her. By digging my heels
in the ground, leaning against her shoulder, and shouting,
"Whoa, Jade, *whoa*!" I eventually stopped her and plodded
back to stand on the mat, shaking my head apologetically

to the others, who were all doubled up laughing.

"Okay." Zak was grinning too. "This time we take one of the mats away so you'll have to be a lot quicker, Caitlin."

I tried not to think how gorgeous he looked and nodded. We're fast learners, Jade and I, and by the third lot of music we were really competing, in a smooth rhythm of canter, halt, dismount, run. Millie was the first to be eliminated, choosing the same mat as Andy, who outran her easily. Next to go was Jacob, who slid off his piebald pony's back so fast he fell over before he could even start running.

"I wouldn't mind"—he gazed up at us ruefully—"but Lucas couldn't care less we're out. Look at him!"

The black-and-white cob had simply taken the opportunity for a spot of grazing, practically stepping over his rider on the way. I was beginning to feel quite fired up, the strong competitive spirit I knew existed flaring into a definite spark within me. There were now only three mats and four of us in, and the second the music stopped I flung myself out of the saddle and sprinted to the nearest mat, Jade trotting at my shoulder. I made it onto the mat a fraction before Corinne arrived with Teddy and grinned at her triumphantly.

"That's not fair," she said instantly. "Caitlin's not holding her horse's reins."

"Jade's right here next to me, though," I defended myself.

"It's not in the rules." Corinne stuck out her lower lip. "Is it, Zak?"

He shrugged helplessly. "I've never seen anyone do it like that but Caitlin's right—she's on the mat and her horse is with her."

"I think the rules say you have to *lead* your pony," Tasha said. "But no one made that clear so you can't eliminate Caitlin. And it was brilliant the way Jade followed her."

"Yeah, but if it's not in the rules—" Corinne persisted.

Andy suggested quickly, "Let's do it again, only this time Caitlin leads her horse same as the rest of us."

"Seems fair." Zak smiled at me. "Okay with you?"

"Sure." I stepped off the mat and remounted.

This time the music played for over three circuits be-

fore Tasha, with her back to us so she couldn't see our po-
sitions, switched it off. I ran like the wind, Jade's reins
hooked over one finger, and reached the mat safely.
Corinne had gone for the same one as Tom and he beat
her to it easily, standing on its center with arms folded.

"Hard luck, Corinne," Zak said easily. She smiled at
him, unable to resist that fabulous combination of blue
eyes and white teeth.

I climbed back aboard again, thinking wryly that it
looked like I was going to have to join a queue when it
came to being smitten by Zak! I concentrated on the
game, trying to shave nanoseconds off my time as I sprang
from the saddle, but the guys were faster, claiming the last
two mats way before I did, leaving me eliminated. Tom
went on to win and got a round of applause as his reward.

"Are you all getting into the spirit of the thing?" Zak's
eyes were twinkling. "Because now you're going to compete as teams. Get yourselves sorted into two sets of three
and come on over here."

To my surprise Tom moved purposefully toward me.
"Will you be in my team, Caitlin?"

"Oh yeah," I said, flattered. "But I'm rubbish—don't know a thing."

"You're a natural," he said. "So who else shall we have?"

"'Fraid you've got me," Millie said in a small voice. "Andy, Jacob, and Corinne have already teamed up."

"Great." Tom was incredibly good-natured, not seeming to mind getting the two duffers at all. "Let's see what the first game is."

It was a flag race, the first team rider galloping across the field to plant a flag into a bucket, then racing back to the start so the second could take off and place his flag and so on. Tom was first to go in our team, flying across the grass with Fenton looking like a steel-gray arrow. He barely slowed as they curved around the bucket, leaning out of the saddle to drop the flag neatly while one-handedly guiding his horse in a smooth canter, then picking up the pace for the gallop back. Millie and Chas took off like a rocket. They were ahead of Jacob in the other team when she reached the end, but she had to slow the overanxious Chas right down before she could place her flag, allowing Jacob's piebald pony to catch up. They were neck and neck as they raced back, and Jade and I took off just a fraction after Corinne and Teddy.

My wonderful pony is fast, though, and we'd pulled ahead and were leading by two strides as I neck reined her round the bucket. Trying too hard, I stood up in the stirrups and dropped my flag from a height. It landed squarely and accurately but before I could complete our turn and race triumphantly back, the bucket tottered and swayed, tipping out the three flags and rolling across the grass. I threw myself to the ground and gathered up the flags, sticking them back in and returning the upright bucket to its proper place—but of course I'd wasted loads of time. Corinne had placed her flag safely and was already halfway back to her teammates—we'd lost.

"I'm sorry," I wailed as Jade and I cantered back. "I completely blew it."

"Don't worry about it—we'll get them next time," Tom promised.

That wasn't quite true. During the next game Millie lost the lead Tom had given us when Chas shied, but after that we just scraped a win in the hectic bending contest.

Another marginal victory for us in the more sedate egg-and-spoon race meant the two teams were drawn.

"We'll do the bride-and-groom race as a decider," Zak announced. "It's designed for teams of four so I'll join Tom's side and Tasha will be on Andy's."

I saw Andy's and Jacob's faces light up immediately at the thought of being joined by Tasha, while Millie was practically dancing because she'd be with Zak. It was a fast and furious game involving a lot of vaulting, so we all had a few minutes' practice beforehand. Millie and I stood on a line way across the field waiting for our "grooms" to rescue us. Zak came first, galloping on the stunning black Jet, and Millie, trembling with excitement, sprang lightly up behind him. A curving turn and they were galloping back to the start with Millie curled blissfully against Zak. Once they crossed the line Tom and Fenton were off, hurtling flat-out toward us. Like I'd told Zak, I've been happily vaulting onto Jade's back for years but I'd never done it at this speed and certainly never swung up behind another rider this way. Tom knew I was worrying and slowed his horse's pace, helping to steady me as I leapt up and across Fenton's back.

"That was good," I panted as I slid to the ground at the finish. "But you needn't slow it so much. I can do it, I know I can."

"Good on you, Caitlin." Zak grinned at me. "You're a real competitor, it comes naturally to you."

We had a few more practice vaults, then Zak called the two teams together and set the contest up for real. Millie, Corinne, and I set off across the field, accompanied by Tasha.

"You're doing really well," she said to me, smiling and tossing back her long switch of hair. "And so are you, Millie. You and Chas are ten times better than last year. I know Zak thinks so."

"*Does* he?" Millie's eyes were glowing, and I thought uneasily that Tasha would realize how keen the younger girl was.

"Don't get carried away, Millie," Corinne said sharply. "Zak just told *me* how well I was doing too."

"I'm sure he thinks highly of all of you," Tasha said easily. "Okay, here we are, get ready to be rescued, girls! Who's going first?"

"Me," Millie said at once. "If that's all right with you, Caitlin?"

"Sure." I knew how much she enjoyed cuddling into Zak. "I'll wait back here for my turn."

Tasha and I moved out of the way, making sure we left plenty of room for the first two "grooms" on their galloping horses. Squinting back at the start I was surprised to see Tom lining up first for our team and I heard Zak's voice shout, "One–two–three–GO!" Fenton and Blaze sprang immediately into action with Tom heading straight for Millie while Andy went flat-out toward Corinne. There was little in it, both girls vaulting expertly behind the two riders as the horses curved round to gallop back down the field. Tasha and I ran back to the "bride" places, both posed and ready. Zak and Jet started slightly behind Jacob on the piebald Lucas but they made up the difference with ease and had pulled ahead when they reached me. I misjudged my leap slightly so that Zak had to check his horse, taking a wider turn before we started on the return ride. Tasha, athletic and graceful, performed a perfect spring, enabling Jacob to regain the lead. They were several meters ahead, galloping strongly to the finish line. Curved against Zak's strong, muscular body, I felt Jet surge forward, his long, powerful stride eating up the ground beneath us until we were alongside the piebald. Tasha's beautiful hair streamed out behind her and she was laughing as we passed. I saw the wicked, conspiratorial grin Zak gave her, and when we came to a triumphant halt the first thing he did was go over and hug her. I stayed with Jet, stroking his gleaming shoulder and trying not to look at the laughing, happy couple.

"Well *done*, Caitlin." Zak took his horse's reins and patted my shoulder casually. "I went all-out for that win and you coped really well."

I mumbled something about not getting it quite right but now Millie had joined us and she was saying nice things too.

"You're already better than me and I've been practicing for a whole year," Millie ended ruefully.

"Um—sorry about you not getting Zak that time." I kept my voice low. "I thought he was riding the first run, not Tom."

"It's okay, so did I," she said, sighing theatrically. "Isn't he just *fabulous*?"

"Er—yes, he's a terrific rider," I said cautiously. "Did you see the way we went past poor old Lucas?"

"Yeah, and Zak was flirting with Tasha at the time." Millie sighed again. "They're so loved up, those two, it makes you sick."

"You don't seem to mind her, though." I was still experiencing shameful pangs of jealousy, as though someone was turning a knife between my ribs, every time Zak and Tasha were together. Millie must be a lot more sensible than me, I thought, or maybe she was just plain nicer.

"No point in minding, is there?" she said cheerfully. "Let's face it, Zak's never going to choose me instead of her. But I can dream, can't I?"

I smiled at her, wondering whether to tell her that by now I was totally knocked out by Zak, too.

"I just live in hope that Tasha's temper will let her down during our holiday," Millie went on. "It would be just lovely if I became the only girl here who felt about him that way."

I opened my mouth to say that wouldn't be the case, then closed it again. I really liked Millie—she was so up-beat and buoyant and she seemed to like me too—so I didn't want to ruin our budding friendship by spoiling her daydreams.

"How you doing, teammates?" Tom had brought our horses over. "*Victorious* teammates, I should say."

"Yeah, good, enjoyed it, thanks." I smiled at him. "Though I'm going to need a lot more practice."

"I'll give you a hand if you like." He swung into his saddle. "Your horse could be a real star at this, you're already so in tune with each other."

"Thanks, but maybe I'm not so good with people! Is Corinne still mad at me?"

"Nah, she's fine, she's just one of those fussy types. She's got Andy and Jacob running round after her so she's quite happy."

"Really?" I looked over to where the other team were still in a huddle. "I thought they were both keen on Tasha."

"Different thing altogether. Tasha's well out of their league—it's like Millie fancying Zak, it's never going to happen. Look, the bending poles are still in place, d'you want another go at them?"

"Yeah." I liked the fact that while I was riding I had to concentrate.

As we moved across the field I saw Ed come into the field.

"He'll watch us all practicing but he won't get involved," Tom explained. "He and Val do all the formal stuff, from dressage through to cross-country, but they leave Zak in charge of mounted games."

"If you want extra tutoring you stick to Tom," Millie advised, riding past. "I need Zak to help me."

"He's all yours," I said lightly, quite proud of the way I was hiding my feelings.

It was better being with Tom anyway because I felt comfortable with him and didn't feel all self-conscious and useless like I did when I was trying to impress Zak. Tom helped me improve my vaulting technique and showed Jade and me how to speed up in the bending.

"She loves it." I slowed my pony after her brilliant display of snaking between the poles. "I reckon she could do it without a rider."

"I'd like to see that," Tom laughed.

So of course I dismounted at once. "Come on Jade." I ran back toward the poles, and she trotted eagerly behind me.

I ran between the first two, right-hand turn, left-hand turn, with Jade at my shoulder, then pointed to the third and said, "GO!" She immediately curved to the left and, while I ran straight along the line of poles, calling to her, she ducked obligingly between them, her timing and technique absolutely perfect.

"Clever girl." I hugged her ecstatically at the end of the line. "You are definitely the best pony in the whole world."

"Incredible!" Tom's mouth was still hanging open. "You've got to show everyone that!"

"D'you think?" A big part of me wanted Zak to give me that same look of stunned admiration.

"Definitely." Tom looked across the field where the others were grouped. "Oh, hang on, it sounds like they've got trouble."

I could hear raised voices now and as I hopped back into my saddle I saw Ed lift his hands despairingly skyward. He turned and started walking away but Tasha chased after him, grabbing his arm and shouting. I couldn't hear what she was saying but it was obvious the infamous temper had flared and Zak's girlfriend was kicking off in a big, big way!

Chapter Five

I was a bit surprised Tom didn't go charging off across the field to see what was going on.

"I'm not keen on rows." He looked at me apologetically. "So I'd rather keep out of the way till they sort themselves out. You don't mind, do you?"

"Not me," I said fervently. "I feel the same way. Millie looks as though she's in the thick of it, though."

I could see her standing next to Zak, and as I watched he handed her Jet's reins and walked over to Tasha, who was now stamping her way back from the gate.

"I should think that's the end of this morning's session," Tom said. "Zak will be running around after Tasha now so we might as well walk the horses back to the yard."

"Okay," I agreed. "Jade deserves a good long rest after all the hard work she's put in this morning."

"And we've got the beach ride later," Tom said, as if I *needed* reminding.

"I'm really looking forward to it and I know you're going to love it too." It was half an hour later and I was still rubbing Jade's back and chatting to her. "You enjoyed this morning but you're going to have the best time ever when you start swimming in the sea."

"Don't get your hopes up!" Millie's face appeared at the stable door. "That's what the row was all about."

"The one between Tasha and Ed?" I looked at her. "What's that got to do with the beach?"

"Well, I don't know exactly." Millie was obviously enjoying a good gossip. "But from what I heard it's something to do with having to ride over next door's land."

"Next door's—?" I shook my head. "Why would Tasha be rowing with Ed over something like that?"

"You don't know her," she said darkly. "Tasha can argue about *anything*."

"So you said." I carried on massaging my pony's back. "What exactly happened to set her off?"

"Well." Millie came in to join me. "Ed said something to Zak about this afternoon's ride and Zak said he'd definitely need some help. There are four of you whose horses have never swum so Zak was saying it would be safer with two instructors."

"Won't Tasha be helping him?" I was under the impression they did everything together.

"That's what Ed assumed. He threw out some remark about it and Tasha just blew up. She said to him, 'You know how I feel about the Grants; you can't possibly expect me to go.' Ed looked a bit shocked and muttered something about this not being the time or the place to discuss it and then he started walking away."

"We saw Tasha run after him." I flexed my aching fingers. "She was really screaming by then."

"I know! Zak tried to quiet her down but she swore at him as well."

"So what happened next?" I tidied everything back into my grooming box. "Tom and I just pushed off out the way."

"Ed kept on walking, completely ignoring Tasha, so she stomped back, grabbed Sabrina, and took off. Zak sort of groaned and hesitated, then he said, 'Sorry, guys, let me just get this sorted,' and he went after her."

"What did he say when he came back?" I gave Jade one last pat and left her to enjoy her lunch.

"That's just it." Millie paused dramatically at the door. "He didn't. Come back, I mean. The four of us just hung around till Val came rushing over. She was all apologetic, said to bring the horses back here and they'd get something sorted for this afternoon. Apparently she and Ed have an appointment so they can't come with us."

"D'you think that means we won't get our ride to the beach this afternoon?" I felt a sickening lurch, a double whammy of disappointment—no swim, no Zak.

Millie shrugged. "Val said they'd try, but I don't know—last year there was only Tasha helping Zak with the fun stuff like games and rides to the beach. Ooh shush—here he comes, look!"

Zak was riding into the yard, his expression hooded

and somber. He slid to the ground and led Jet into his stable. I was all for getting out of the way again but Millie hung on to my arm so we were still in the yard when Zak reappeared.

"Hi," Millie said with artificial brightness. "Um—Caitlin was just asking about the beach ride. It's still on, is it?"

"Yes." For the first time he didn't switch on the fabulous smile. "We meet here at three thirty. Make sure you've got your swimming stuff."

"Right, thanks," we both stammered as we watched him slope away.

"Phew." Millie let out her breath in a long sigh. "Does he look bad-tempered or what! I bet you Tasha's still playing him up."

"Looks like it," I agreed, thinking passionately that he deserved someone better. "But at least the beach ride's still on."

"You just can't wait, can you?" Millie laughed. "I hope it's not a massive letdown like my first experience was."

We spent the time after we'd eaten chilling out in the

garden again. Corinne, Andy, and Jacob were also greatly looking forward to their first swim.

"Lucas *has* actually tried before," Jacob told us. "In a river at home, but it wasn't that deep really and I think he was just making it up."

"You mean bending his knees and pretending his hooves were off the ground?" Corinne mocked him. "As if!"

"What about you and Teddy then?" Andy was very flirty with her. "Have you done anything more than paddle?"

"No, but Teddy will be a natural." She tossed her blond hair about. "I just know it."

"I hope Jade is," I said fervently. "We've never done anything like it before."

"You hadn't done games either and you were both brilliant at that," Tom said encouragingly. "I mean, our team beat this lot, didn't we?"

That set everyone off in a lighthearted battle and we ended up tearing round the garden hurling armfuls of mown grass at each other. Millie and I spent a good ten minutes afterward picking bits of green out of Corinne's pretty hair till we all flaked out again and lay under the trees swapping funny stories about our lives and our riding. It was the first time I could remember feeling part of a group like this, and I found myself relaxing and thoroughly enjoying the experience. I still wanted to see my Best Friend Jade, of course, so half an hour or so before we were due back in the yard, I slipped away from the others so I could spend some time with her.

She'd eaten all her lunch and was drowsily resting in the cool shelter of her stable, but she gave an immediate whicker of pleasure when I opened the door. I gave her a cuddle and told her what I'd been doing, stroking her gently so that she closed her eyes and leaned against me. Gently untangling some strands of her mane, I kept my voice low so as not to disturb the lovely serenity of the stable block, and got quite a shock when a sudden, strident voice shattered the peace.

"So what you're saying is, you support your parents rather than me. Thanks for nothing, Zak!"

It was Tasha, and though I was hidden from view in a

corner well back from the door, and couldn't see her, I could clearly imagine the explosive fury on her face.

"Oh come on, Tasha." Zak sounded weary and very fed up. "It's not like that, you know it isn't. I'm part of the family business so I have to stand by my dad's decisions."

"Even though he's practically calling me a liar?" A door clicked shut and I realized she was in the adjoining stall with Sabrina.

"He's not calling you a liar, he's just accepting the situation as he sees it." Zak had followed her in.

"Yeah right. He believes Ray Grant's telling the truth and I'm not—it's the same thing."

"No it isn't. Grant has proof, Dad says, and the fact you don't believe in it doesn't make you a liar—just mistaken that's all."

"Mistaken!" Her voice went an octave higher. "I'm not mistaken about the way he cheated my uncle over a property deal last year, am I? You knew about that and yet you're on your parents' side, not mine."

"It's not a question of sides." Zak was obviously losing patience. "The coast ride is an important part of the holidays we offer. I can't go shooting my mouth off at the neighbors when I've got nothing to support what you're saying."

"So we're back to square one, you'd rather stick with your family and your business than me, even though if I'm right—"

"You see," he interrupted harshly, "you're saying *if*. Admit that you're not a hundred percent sure about this, Tasha. You just don't like Ray Grant and you're using this obsession to try and start some sort of feud."

"It's not an obsession! My uncle's got firsthand knowledge of his dishonesty, and that makes me suspicious of the way Grant *conveniently* discovered his so-called evidence. You and your family are far too trusting—oh, we're never going to agree about this, so maybe I'd better just go, Zak."

"You can't go," he said flatly. "You're booked to take the beach ride with me. You were happy enough to take this on as a summer job when my parents offered you, so you *have* to honor it."

"That was different," she flared again. "It was before—"

"Before you started rowing with Ray Grant." His voice became fainter as he moved away. "You're always fighting with *someone*, Tasha, just get over it will you!"

As his footsteps faded I distinctly heard Tasha start to cry and wondered briefly whether I should say something. My dislike of any sort of emotional confrontation made me stay quiet and I was highly relieved when, after several loud sniffs, she too walked out of the stable, closing and bolting the door behind her. After a few minutes I risked peeking out and was very pleased to see an empty, quiet yard once more. It would soon be time for the others to arrive and start getting their horses ready for the afternoon ride—if, after what I'd just overheard, it was actually going to take place. I fetched Jade's tack and grooming kit and returned to her stable just as Tom appeared.

"I wondered where you'd gotten to." He grinned at me cheerfully. "I should have guessed you were here!"

"Mm." I wished I knew him well enough to confide I'd been unintentionally eavesdropping. "I was just keeping Jade company for a bit."

"Have you been discussing tactics for your swim?" he

86

teased, holding the door open for me.

"Nah. Everyone says she'll either love it straight-off or—"

"Or she won't." Millie had arrived. "I'm just hoping Chas will remember how much he loved it last year. It took a while but we got there eventually, didn't we, Zak?"

"That's right." The brilliance had gone from his blue eyes, and it was an obvious effort to smile. "Is everyone here?"

I found I was digging my fingernails into the palm of my hand, willing him not to say the ride was canceled.

"Yeah, here we are." Corinne, Andy, and Jacob rushed over to get their saddles, and I relaxed and tried to feel more hopeful.

There was no sound coming from the stable next to mine and it wasn't until I was tightening Jade's girth that I heard Tasha go in and speak quietly to her pony. I led Jade into the yard, and, what with feeling slightly apprehensive about the ride and *very* nervous about Tasha's temper, I was more than usually subdued.

"Don't worry, Caitlin." Millie thought it was just rid-

ing nerves. "You'll be fine even if you do fall off. It does-
n't hurt—you just get a bit wet that's all."

"I haven't fallen off for years." Corinne tucked her hair
carefully under her hat. "And neither has Andy. We were
just talking about it."

"I fall off a *lot*," Jacob said ruefully. "So I'm expecting
to get pretty soaked."

"Hopefully not." Zak was already up on Jet. "But if any
of you do come off, can you please try and hold on to your
horse's reins? It'll be hard for me to keep an eye on everyone if I'm chasing after loose ponies all the time."

"You talk as though you're taking this ride out on your
own." Tasha led out the pretty palomino Sabrina.

"I—um—" The look he gave her was an almost comic
mixture of relief, gratitude, and exasperation. "No, of
course not. Tasha will be there to help, of course."

"Of course," she repeated, swinging easily into the saddle. "It's my job, it's what I'm paid for."

I saw Tom blink, but no one else, not even Millie,
seemed to notice the tension between the two. I crossed
my fingers superstitiously and hoped everything was going

to be all right. We rode out in a line of twos, with Zak and me leading, followed by Corinne and Andy, then Tom and Millie, with an ecstatic-looking Jacob bringing up the rear with Tasha. At first we followed the track we'd taken the day before but when it divided into two we took the right-hand fork, cantering along a broad swath of grass bordered by a row of heavy-duty fencing. Zak, still deep in thought and uncommunicative, checked the route ahead and held up a hand to show we were slowing. A young man, loading wooden posts onto a pickup truck, waved a greeting.

"Off to the cove then?" His thin face was very tanned.

"Uh-huh." Zak nodded. "We've got four new guests among this group, and they're all keen to swim."

"Is that right? Make sure you warn them to stay away from Tiber Cliffs. There was another fall last week."

"Will do, thanks. See you later." As he led us away, Zak gave me the first proper smile of the afternoon, so I felt encouraged enough to speak.

"Why did the man say that?"

"Paul? Oh, about the cliff you mean?"

"Yes. Has someone fallen down into the sea from where

you showed us yesterday?"

He laughed, his face relaxing at last. "No, don't worry, Caitlin. Paul's a keen fisherman, always out in his boat, and it's rockfalls he's warning about. Nothing serious, but it makes sense for us to keep away from that part of the bay."

"Oh, right," I said, relieved. "Where are we going now?"

Keeping to the line of the high fence, Zak was leading us toward us a heavy metal gate.

"Our route takes us across the edge of a neighbor's land," he said, not looking at me. "He's very kindly allowing us to ride through his property. I'll open the gate so you can ride in, then just wait till I rejoin you. Okay?"

"Okay." I kept my voice and my expression noncommittal.

We were obviously entering the grounds belonging to Ray Grant, the neighbor about whom Tasha had quarreled so violently with Ed. I did exactly as Zak said, walking sedately through the open gate, then bringing Jade to a decorous halt a few meters the other side. I was itching to turn round and see how Tasha was reacting but thought I'd let Millie tell me later—she was bound to be watching for any possible fireworks! Zak still seemed tense as we rode quietly along the tree-lined track. There was no sign of a house, so I imagined it must be farther over to our right, but as we moved forward the salty tang of the air became more pronounced and soon I could hear the wonderful sound of the sea. We emerged from the trees onto a stretch of scrubby-looking grass that quickly gave way to dark, coarse sand, graduating into the fine, pale gleam of beach we'd seen from the day before. Once again I drew in my breath as I took in the view—the sweeping curve of the bay, encircled by towering cliffs of slate gray, the gentle waves lapping on the shore while ocean breakers threw up clouds of white spray farther out among some rocks. And the sea itself, an endless, rhythmic mass of deep blue, shading into azure, cobalt, and turquoise. I exhaled at last, feeling Jade twitch and prance beneath me, filled with the same excitement and wonder.

"Like it?" Zak's gorgeous eyes smiled into mine.

"It's—it's—" I couldn't speak.

"Come and get a closer look." He twisted in his saddle to check everyone was okay. "We'll start off along the beach so your horses get a nice gradual introduction. Let them take their time to look; it's a whole new experience so it might take them a while to settle when we get nearer the water."

We flowed gradually into a gentle canter and I could hear the ponies behind me snorting and plunging in their excitement. Even my usually well-mannered Jade was hard to hold, bursting with enthusiasm at the glorious new sensation of sand beneath her hooves and sea air in her nostrils. When we reached the slightly damp, firmer ground at the ocean's edge she was desperate to gallop. I could feel her energy fizzing all around me and had to hang on tight to keep her under control.

Zak grinned his approval at me then yelled, "Okay, let's give them a nice pipe-opener—just a short gallop, everyone."

We took off like a bunch of racehorses, plunging from canter into the exhilarating four-time beat, and I laughed with sheer joy as Jade stretched every muscle in an effort to keep up with the awesome speed of Zak's Thorough-bred. She nearly made it, her pretty bay head getting closer and closer to Jet's gleaming black shoulder until Zak raised his hand again, curving his horse in a smooth arc before we reached the towering cliffs ahead. The action took us back along the sweep of the bay and meant we'd ridden toward the shoreline so were now cantering powerfully through the edge of the sea itself, our horses' hooves kicking up spray that cascaded in a million shining drops around us. We dropped the pace further and, well before we neared the rocky outcrop at the other end of the bay, our horses were walking, splashing their way pastern-deep through the crystal-clear waves beneath them.

"Give Jade a long rein so she can investigate." Zak was smiling at my overjoyed expression. "But be careful she doesn't decide to roll. It's caught out plenty of riders before today."

I watched my pony's intelligent eyes take in the vista, laughing as she reached down and blew curiously at the strange, salty element swirling around her feet.

"Ooh!" Corinne shrieked. "Teddy's pawing at the

water—is he going to lie down?"

"Keep him moving if you think he might." Tasha, still unsmiling, rode close to her. "How are the rest of you doing?"

"Great." Millie was grinning from ear to ear. "I think Chas is going to be all right, Zak."

"Good." He moved Jet farther into the waves. "We'll take their saddles off soon so you can give him a try."

Tom, on the super-cool Fenton, was also wading knee-deep and I asked Jade to follow, not sure what she'd make of it. She joined him at once, seeming to revel in the feel of the cool water around her legs.

"Hey, not too deep, Caitlin," Zak called out. "You nearly got wet boots just then."

All the horses seemed to be enjoying their first experience of the ocean, so after a while Zak said we could untack and get ready to go in a little deeper. I literally couldn't wait and, having whipped off Jade's saddle plus my boots and breeches, had vaulted aboard her bare back before anyone else had finished stowing their things on some dry rocks farther up the beach.

"Wait for me." Tom hopped effortlessly onto Fenton. "You've still got your T-shirt on anyway."

Being pretty shy, I'd deliberately worn a baggy number that covered my swimsuit.

"I don't suppose I'll get it wet," I said quickly. "Jade probably won't want to go in that deep, so it's only if I fall in."

"*That* is always a possibility." Millie was clambering back on Chas. "And if I had a figure like yours I wouldn't cover it up anyway."

I poked my tongue out at her and glanced quickly round, wondering if Zak had heard. Stripped to a pair of shorts he was one heck of a gorgeous sight but his whole attention was focused on Tasha, who, still pouting and sulky, looked a total knockout in a skimpy bikini. Zak's eyes said it all: Despite the aggravation she was causing him he was utterly besotted. Still, I told myself irritably, now was not the time for me to get an attack of jealousy—now was the first time ever I was going to swim in the sea with Jade. Taking a deep breath, I moved her forward—we were on our way to the shining, moving mass of that ocean!

Chapter Six

Tom rode beside me, both he and his horse appearing very laid-back and cool about the whole thing. I, on the other hand, was practically shaking with anticipation, and Jade was prancing and snorting excitedly.

"Calm down a bit, you two," Tom said, grinning at me. "You're like a rocket about to explode."

I breathed deeply and tried to relax as we walked into the shallow edge of the sea. Here, on the shoreline, it lapped gently, almost lazily, each wave outlined with a fine, lacy foam. With every step I could feel its power increase, swirling strongly round my pony's legs as she and Fenton moved into deeper water. The sea now reached her shoulder and I was loving the feel of cool, silky water on my bare feet and legs. We'd reached the coastal shelf, the point where many horses refuse to go any farther, but I knew my own wonderful pony. She and I felt completely attuned, moving through this glorious new element as if we'd been born to it.

And then, suddenly, "You're swimming!" Tom said.

I couldn't reply; the amazing sensation as Jade moved powerfully, easily through the deep blue of the ocean completely took my breath away. It was like being astride a dolphin, every muscle in her wet, shining body rippling beneath me. The waves, stronger out here, swelled around us and she breasted them joyfully, swimming into each one with effortless ease.

"God, she's good!" After a while Tom was struggling to keep up with us. "I thought Fenton was at home in the water but your horse must be part fish!"

"Jade's a sea horse," I called back dreamily. "It feels as though she could do this forever."

"Yeah, well, I hate to break the mood, but you'd better not. We can't go any farther or any deeper. Can't you hear Zak yelling?"

"Oh?" I shook my head in an effort to return to reality.

Zak was indeed yelling so I obediently turned my pony, reveling in the way she responded, and began swimming back the way we'd come. I hadn't realized just how far we'd traveled; the others seemed quite a distance away, with three horses swimming fairly close to the shoreline while the other three were still in the shallows.

"Millie and Chas are doing okay." Tom pointed to the girl's dark head.

Chas was very close to Zak's horse, looking like a wet, roasted chestnut against the sleek brilliant black of Jet. Lucas was swimming too, his chunky piebald body cutting beautifully through the water while a delighted Jacob whooped with glee.

"He can do it! My horse can swim!"

"He's great," I called back, waving madly.

We'd nearly reached the trio and Zak said sarcastically, "Well, thanks for joining us, you two! I thought you were heading for the open sea the way you were going!"

"Sorry." I brought Jade alongside. "Tom had to remind

me about not going out of the bay or too near Tiber Cliffs."

"Didn't you realize how far you'd gotten?" Millie was slithering about a bit on her horse's wet back. "I've never seen a horse go so fast in water."

"Jade's a natural," I said proudly.

Zak gave me a reluctant, but still gorgeous, smile. "She sure is, but don't go mad. This is a safe, sheltered bay but it's a different story beyond those cliffs."

"Okay, I'll be careful." I was actually feeling wild and reckless for once but I knew he was right. "How are Corinne and Andy doing?"

"Not too good." Millie tried not to giggle. "Darling Teddy won't go in any deeper than his knees, and Blaze is pretty spooked too."

As we watched Tasha tried leading Corinne's pony forward, getting Sabrina to walk confidently into the deeper water. The bay Teddy took two steps then stopped dead, nearly dragging Tasha off her horse's back. She patiently turned the palomino and went back, this time getting close behind Teddy and trying to push him.

"Leave him for now," Zak called out to her. "Corinne, just get him to relax and enjoy a paddle while Tasha tries Blaze again."

"I can't understand why he's being so naughty," Corinne yelled back. "He usually does everything I ask."

"Don't worry, some horses need to take their time. Try leading Andy in, would you, Tasha?"

His girlfriend gave him a withering look and silently took hold of Blaze's reins. With a lot of positive riding and encouragement the chestnut horse slowly moved forward. At the point where the seabed shelved into deep water he threw on the brakes briefly, but Sabrina kept going. Andy stayed calm but firm till Blaze suddenly capitulated, joining the palomino to swim through the gentle swell of the waves.

"Great. Well done, Andy." Zak turned Jet toward Tasha. "And—um—thanks, honey."

"Oh, I'm honey now, am I?" She almost spat out the words, and I saw Zak's shoulders sag.

We all pretended we hadn't heard but I saw the way Millie looked and knew she was feeling the same sympathy for Zak and dislike for Tasha that I was.

"Try swimming alongside Jade for change." Tom lightened the mood by sliding off Fenton's back into the water. "It's good fun."

My T-shirt was already soaked so I joined him, kicking my legs hard to keep up with my horse.

"She's too fast for me." Within minutes I was gasping. "I'm just being towed along."

"If I get off I'll never get back on!" Millie shrieked, but she flopped into the sea anyway.

Jacob was the best in the water, doing an effortless backstroke while Lucas swam happily beside him.

"Come on, Corinne." Zak had given up trying to placate his girlfriend. "Try again. Teddy might be keener now all his friends are out here."

Corinne did everything she could and actually managed to get her horse almost chest-deep.

"You're practically there!" Zak was all encouragement. "One more push!"

I heard Tasha mutter something irritable as she turned Sabrina toward the shore. "I'll give you another lead,

Corinne," she called impatiently. "Get ready."

"I don't think—" Zak began.

Again she flashed him a look that would freeze a hot dog so he shut up. Sabrina, swimming strongly, approached Teddy, and Tasha leaned over and grabbed a rein. "Now push! Go on, lots of leg!"

Poor Corinne did her best and for a while it looked as though they'd won, with the bay horse nearly making the deeper water, but at the last moment he stopped dead and jerked his head defiantly back. Tasha didn't stand a chance, having been surging forward one-handed on the slippery wet back of her pony; she was yanked through the air to fall with a resounding splash directly in front of Teddy. He reacted by half rearing in the water, dumping Corinne practically on top of the other girl, then spinning round to wade back into the shallows and up onto the beach.

Zak was amazingly quick off the mark, riding Jet after the fleeing horse immediately. The rest of us watched openmouthed as Tasha, her gorgeous red hair plastered like a strand of old wet rope down her back, swam after her own horse. I managed to move Jade quickly enough to block the palomino's route and leaned over to catch her reins and bring her alongside. Tasha swam toward us and clambered silently onto Sabrina's back. She always wore makeup, I'd noticed, but now it had run and was streaked down her face. Her eyelashes, without mascara, looked stubby and pale.

"Thank you," she said stiffly. I had to try really hard not to smirk.

Corinne, her own carefully coiffed hair hanging in rats' tails around her face, was plodding back to shore.

"No one's hurt, that's the important thing," Millie said in a high, artificially bright voice. I knew she was trying not to laugh as well.

Zak had caught Teddy and was leading him back through the sea's edge toward Corinne.

"I think we'd better join them," Tom muttered.

Andy, who'd only had a short swim, was already pointing Blaze shoreward; as soon as he reached it he jumped down to comfort Corinne. She was remarkably philosophical about the incident, thanking Zak for rescuing Teddy and even apologizing for letting him go.

"The reins just slipped out of my hands—well, actually Tasha pulled them—so I couldn't hang on to him like you said."

"Don't worry." Zak still hadn't risked looking at his girl-friend. "Your horse will definitely go in another day—he just isn't ready yet."

While we were all toweling ourselves and our horses down, Zak and Tasha moved farther along the beach where it was obvious another argument was taking place.

"She's giving him a hard time because *she* was stupid enough to get a soaking," Millie said indignantly. "It was her own fault!"

"Yeah maybe." I thought strongly that Tasha should stop sulking, stop yelling, and start being supportive to her fabulous boyfriend, but I was still trying to keep my feelings for him hidden. "She was pretty upset before we even got here so we shouldn't be too hard on her."

Millie said a rude word that everyone heard, but it sounded so funny coming from her we all burst out laughing.

"Glad to hear everyone's still happy." Zak came over to

join us.

He looked far from happy himself, the tense, worried expression etched even more deeply on his handsome face.

The sun was very warm in this lovely sheltered cove and, combined with a gentle sea breeze, soon dried the horses as we lazed on the beach. Corinne was able to stuff her uncharacteristically messy hair under her riding helmet, and we all saddled up for the ride back. Tasha had cleared the streaks of makeup from her face but was looking tired and depressed. The magnificent cascade of her hair was still damp, staining her shirt with seawater, and she remained silent and aloof from the rest of us. Zak led the way across the beach onto the grass, this time accompanied by a very animated and talkative Millie. Jacob, after several attempts at conversation with Tasha, rode Lucas alongside Tom and me.

"Tasha's having a major sulk," he said in a stage whisper. "And I think she'd rather be left alone."

The broad track was easily wide enough to ride together. Even when we saw a tall figure striding toward us we didn't have to split up.

"Afternoon, Zak." The man nodded curtly. "All of these people are your guests, I take it?"

"Yes, Mr. Grant." Zak looked uneasy. "And—er—Tasha of course."

Ray Grant's eyes swiveled in her direction. "Ah yes. And she's been swimming I see."

There was a sudden movement from the girl behind us as, apparently galvanized into action, she rode past us.

"Yes, Ray, I've been swimming. Do I have to pay extra for that? I mean, surely you must own all the water in the sea here as well as all the land surrounding it." Before anyone else could speak she kicked Sabrina into canter. "Send me the bill why don't you?" Her voice floated back and I saw Zak's head slump forward.

"That was entirely uncalled for." Ray Grant looked extremely put out.

"Very sorry," Zak mumbled. "She's upset, I'm sure she didn't mean it."

"And I'm sure she did. Get your father to give me a call, would you?" He turned sharply on his heel and left us.

Zak closed his eyes briefly then repeated dully, "Very

sorry, you guys. We shouldn't be bothering you with all this."

We muttered halfhearted things like "Don't worry" and "It doesn't matter" and carried on along the track, the easy-going atmosphere replaced by an uneasy tension.

Once outside the Grant grounds, Zak carefully secured the gate. "We usually take a longer route back to Beacon Lodge from here, but I'd better go straight there today to—um—"

"That's fine," Tom, seeing his embarrassment, broke in kindly. "We can always ride round your cross-country course if we want extra."

"I think Jade's probably had all the exercise she needs," I added, backing him up. "She was swimming for ages."

"Blaze hasn't done much," Andy began doubtfully, but I nudged him hard and he tactfully subsided.

Zak went straight to the house while we got the hose out and washed the salt off the ponies. Corinne wanted to rush immediately to the shower to sort out her ruined hair so the rest of us gave all the horses, including Teddy and Jet, a thorough rinse.

"What about Sabrina?" I looked into the empty stable. "Has Tasha put her straight into the field d'you think?"

"She's probably taken her home." Tom gently sprayed Fenton's undercarriage. "Her house is only about a mile away."

"Oh? I thought Sabrina lived here all the time." I was scraping excess water from Jade's coat.

"Yeah, she does when things are—" He hesitated. "Normal."

"I don't know her as well as you," Jacob said. "But I'd guess nothing much stays 'normal' for long while Tasha's around."

"She's pretty easy to rile up," Tom agreed. "But last summer it was usually fairly minor and soon over and done with. This year's different—she seems really wound up."

I thought he was being very charitable. As far as I was concerned Tasha's behavior was crass, and the sooner Zak realized it and dumped her the better. I was still keeping a tight hold of my feelings, though, and kept quiet, just concentrating on getting every last bit of salt from irritating Jade's skin.

"Don't they all look gorgeous?" I stood back and admired our handiwork. "We ought to take photos because the minute we turn them out they'll roll and cover themselves in dirt and grass."

"I thought I'd leave Fenton in his box," Tom said. "And maybe take him across the cliffs in a couple of hours to watch the sunset."

"Nice one." I smiled at him. "I don't suppose you fancy some company?"

"You bet." He quickly made up a couple of hay nets for our ponies and we left them contentedly munching while we took the other horses to the field.

Jet hardly got inside the gate before rolling, choosing a bare, dusty patch to squirm blissfully in. His gleaming coat was covered in a powdering of brown earth, and bits of grass stuck out comically in his mane and tail.

"I hope Zak doesn't want to ride later as well," Tom said, laughing. "He's going to have to do some serious brushing if he does!"

"He didn't mention going out, did he?" I kept my voice

casual. "I mean, he's not joining us on the sunset ride, is he?"

"Don't think so." Tom shot me a quizzical look. "You're just stuck with me, I'm afraid."

"Great," I said quickly. "Nice and peaceful, just the way I like it."

"You're not into all this drama then? Heated rows and people flouncing off?"

"Not my scene at all." I hesitated. "But that's just Tasha, isn't it?"

"She's got a fiery temper. Millie and I have seen her blow her top before, but it was always over in a flash. She seems—I don't know—really unhappy this year, genuinely upset I think."

I privately thought she was a spoiled brat who just wanted everything her own way, but I didn't say so. "Mm, maybe. I expect Zak will bring her round, smooth over this row between her and Ray Grant."

"That gate and the fencing around the grounds are all new," he surprised me by saying. "And judging by what Tasha said earlier she's not keen on it."

"Boring stuff." I made a face. "But I wish they'd get it sorted and stop spoiling our riding with it."

"Caitlin!" Millie came thundering toward us. "Thanks for putting Chas out for me."

"No problem." I looked at her curiously. "Where did you go rushing off to so suddenly?"

"I saw Zak coming out of the house so I thought I'd go and casually bump into him."

"Very casual," I said drily. "What did his parents say about Tasha's latest?"

"He was pretty cagey about it but I got the impression his girlfriend isn't too popular with any of them at the moment." She was practically rubbing her hands together with glee. "I reckon Zak will definitely dump her if she makes any more trouble."

"Even if he does it won't mean you stand a chance," Tom pointed out, a bit cruelly I thought. "You're much too young for him for a start."

"Age should not be a barrier," she said with mock dignity. "But seriously, I know I'm not in with a chance or anything but it would be a good thing if he got rid of

Tasha. She only messes everything up. He'd be better off without her."

"You think?" Tom said solemnly.

"Yeah I do, and now she's started fighting with the Grants she's nothing but a liability."

"I'm surprised you haven't gotten the whole story about that," I told her. "Not that I'm interested. Hey we're going for a ride on the cliffs later—d'you want to come?"

"Is Zak going?" she asked immediately.

"No," Tom replied.

"I won't bother then. Tell you what, I'll spend the time finding out all about the Grants."

"Oh goody." I pretended to yawn. "I can't wait."

As it turned out I was glad Millie had decided against joining us. The ride to the clifftop was just fabulous, and the well-matched Fenton and Jade seemed to enjoy it as much as we did. They were fresh and eager to go after their rest and the uphill gallop to the summit was fantastic, the early-evening air soft and cool against the skin as we raced shoulder-to-shoulder along the track. I gasped again when we crested the top and could see the awesome sight of the ocean spreading into the distance. The sun was low in the sky, a ball of fiery red outlined in gold throwing long fingers of color across the darkening sea. In the west a lone sail showed, looking almost black against the brilliant background of sea and sky as it made its way to shore below Tiber Cliffs. We stayed well away from the edge, not wanting a repeat of Jade's skittishness, but in fact her behavior was impeccable.

"This holiday is already doing her good," I told Tom. "She's loved everything we've done and it's making her settled and happier."

"You must have been right when you told me she was a natural sea horse," he said, quite seriously. "Since she's being so good, want to risk a clifftop canter? We only walked last time up here and—"

"Gotcha! Last one to that tree over there is a—a loser." I touched Jade's sides and she took off immediately, leaving Tom and Fenton standing.

"You witch!" He was after me straightaway, laughing out loud as he urged the gray horse forward to catch us.

Shrieking and giggling, I swerved around in front of

them as we pounded across the clifftop that was now
bathed in a deep red glow. I was enjoying our fooling
about so much I wasn't looking ahead properly so when,
against the fading light of the setting sun, a tall figure suddenly appeared in silhouette directly in our path, it seemed
there was no way we could avoid a head-on collision!

Chapter Seven

Luckily, with a bit of neat swerving on our part, both Tom and I managed to avert disaster. I was first to stop, bringing Jade to a slithering halt on the downward slope and turning immediately to check everything was okay.

"Sorry, we just didn't see you—are you all right?"

The man dusted himself down irritably. "Well, you weren't looking, were you? You shouldn't be mucking about like that up here, it's dangerous."

"We did say we were sorry." Tom had brought Fenton back to join me. "I checked the track first and it was clear—you seemed to appear out of nowhere."

He opened his mouth to speak and I said, "It's Paul, isn't it?"

A wary look came into the man's eye. "How d'you know that?"

"We met you this morning, we—"

"I got you. You were with Zak," he nodded. "Oh well, no harm done, apology accepted."

Tom, sounding annoyed, persisted. "So where did you spring up from? Not the main path here, did you climb up the cliff?"

"It's a shortcut from my boat," Paul said reluctantly. "Don't you kids go trying it, though, these cliffs aren't safe."

"Okay, we won't." I wanted to smooth things over. "Thanks for your advice and—um—I hope you enjoyed your fishing."

"No luck today," he mumbled.

"Shame." I was trying too hard.

"I'd better go—oh, you can tell Ed and Val I'll be along to start work tomorrow now I've finished Ray Grant's fence."

"We'll tell them," Tom turned Fenton away. "Come on, Caitlin."

"You were a bit grouchy," I remarked once we were out of earshot. "What did that Paul do to upset you?"

"He was a bit quick to put the blame on us, yet we were the ones who got out of the way." Tom was quite riled up. "Saying that what we were doing was dangerous while *he* was the one clambering about on an unstable cliff!"

The rest of the ride was without incident and wonderfully carefree, cantering through the woods and grassland at the base of the inland line of the cliffs. We reached Beacon Lodge just as the last of the light was fading from the evening sky. Jade and Fenton moved happily through the gate into their field and made us laugh by taking turns to roll in exactly the same spot. They were still together when we went to fetch them the next morning.

"You two are becoming a bit of an item." Tom scratched his pony lovingly between the ears.

"That's nice." Millie, on her way to get Chas, nudged me meaningfully. "Quite a coincidence really!"

"Millie's always fooling around." I put my arms around Jade's neck and breathed in her lovely morning smell. "And half the time I don't know what she's talking about!"

Ed was waiting for us in the outdoor school once we were all tacked up and ready. He looked, I thought, as though he was under a great deal of strain, but his manner was, as always, kind and courteous. We did some warming-up exercises first while he stood in the center of the school and watched closely. There were a number of small jumps set up around us and several of the horses, including Jade, got very excited when they saw them. Jade loves to jump and seems naturally talented, soaring over single obstacles and ditches that we come across when we're out with great ease and style. We haven't done much in the show jumping ring, though, and the few times we tried I found she got faster and faster with each jump until we were tearing round the ring somewhat out of control. I listened carefully to Ed's intelligent teaching and watched the more experienced show jumpers handle the simple, inviting course he'd set out. Andy and Blaze were particularly talented, and I could see the lesson held absolutely no challenge for them.

"Val has an appointment late morning, I'm afraid, but she'll happily instruct you round a cross-country course before she has to go—I know that's what you want to concentrate on." Ed smiled his appreciation of Andy's excellent riding. "Corinne, you and Teddy will probably benefit from that too."

"How about me?" Millie was thrilled to have gotten Chas round the course with no faults.

"I'd like you to work on your approach a little more," Ed told her. "And the same goes for Jacob and Caitlin. Tom, you can join in Val's class if you prefer."

"I'd rather stay here and get Fenton turning more smoothly," Tom said.

"Oh, there's a surprise!" Millie made round, saucer eyes at me. I shook my head, baffled at what she could mean.

I really, *really* enjoyed the lesson, though, working hard at our main problem—maintaining rhythm, something Ed informed us was essential for all successful riding. Jade took the first two jumps, placed on one of the long sides of the school, beautifully but as we turned, making sure we were on the correct leading leg, in a figure-of-eight shape to take two more placed at an angle in the center, she tended to rush, making her unbalanced and spoiling our all-important rhythm. Millie had started to develop the bad habit of dropping her head and looking down.

"Your head is the heaviest part of your body," Ed explained, "so it's a major balancing factor. As soon as you look down your back rounds and your horse's balance is affected, of course. Jacob, your balance is excellent but you're dropping your hands in the last stride before take-off, just at the point where Lucas needs a quiet, steady contact to give him confidence."

Part of Jade's rushing problem was caused by me trying to restrict her during our approach, over-holding and making her tense, so there was plenty for us to work on. It was quite intense but Ed was a great teacher, varying the exercise and methods so that neither horses nor riders got bored. As a reward for all that concentration we took them over to the cross-country area so they could let off some steam with an exuberant canter through the undulating fields and woods. There was a huge expanse of land with two levels of jumps cleverly winding through it.

"A bit more practice in the school and you'll soon be jumping the junior route." Tom pointed to a solidly built wall.

"That doesn't look too bad." I felt quite perky. "But—oh, look at that one over there!"

An arrangement of corner rails, requiring an extremely athletic bounce jump, loomed on the rise of a slope looking, I have to say, absolutely *huge*.

"Yeah, well, next year for that one maybe." Tom grinned at my horrified face. "But I can honestly see you and Jade tackling this course pretty soon."

Showing off a bit, he put Fenton over the wall, cantering on easily to clear a few straw bales stacked some way behind it.

"*We* can do that." Millie bounced about in her saddle. "Come on, Jacob, I'll race you."

"Nah." He was keeping very quiet. "I want to sort out the problem with my hands. I hate the thought I'm putting poor old Lucas off his stride."

"I feel the same way." I smiled apologetically at Millie. "Sorry, I guess you think I'm boring, but I'd like to make sure I'm doing it right before I ask Jade to take this on."

"Let's just have a flat race then," Jacob suggested. "Only

I get to have a head start because my boy doesn't have the natural speed of you lot."

"We'll all need a bit of help if we're racing Caitlin and Jade." Tom rode back to join us. "They're *awesome*."

"*Awesome*," mimicked Millie unkindly. "I don't believe you! One–two–three–GO!"

She was off like a bullet out of a gun, with Chas scorching across the grass away from the three of us. I went after her, laughing out loud at her cheek, and felt a thrill of exultation as Jade stretched into her glorious gallop rhythm. It didn't take long for us to draw level and I deliberately held Jade in line, calling out childish taunts to Millie who groaned as she urged Chas onward. We passed the chestnut horse easily, surging smoothly ahead until we were a length, then two, then three in front—and still accelerating. Thoroughly enjoying ourselves, we swept a wide, sweeping arc around an enormous chair fence before slowing down, a smooth transition through the paces to walk. Tom was the first to reach me, only a few lengths behind; he hadn't been able to top our speed and he now approached, laughing and shaking his fist in mock anger.

"Not fair! You left us at the start!"

"Blame Millie for that, not me." I grinned back at him. "She took off, we just followed, that's all."

The four of us walked back to the start of the course, joking and teasing one another in the easy, friendly way I was really starting to enjoy. Tom wanted to see how Val's lesson was going, and Jacob decided to accompany him.

"I won't join in but it'll be good to watch and see how it should be done." He patted his horse kindly.

I was about to say I'd go along too but Millie leaned over and whispered, "Come and chill out with me. I've got some hot gossip to tell you!"

We watched Tom and Jacob make their way over to the stretch of grass where Val was keeping a close eye on her two students, then sauntered off to a quiet, shady area not far from the house.

"I'll give Jade's back a rest"—I slid to the ground—"while you catch me up with all the latest."

I loosened Jade's girth and ran the stirrup irons up, then smoothed my hand quickly over her legs to check there was no heat in the joints.

"I think this is the end," Millie sighed theatrically. "Or at least the beginning of the end."

Still thinking horse, I stared at her in alarm. "Of Chas you mean?"

"Don't be a dork. Of The Big Romance. Zak and Tasha."

"Yeah?" I tried to look noncommittal.

"Yeah. After yesterday's outburst at Ray Grant she went straight home—hasn't come back, hasn't phoned. And what's more significant—" She paused for dramatic effect. "—Zak hasn't contacted her either. He told me so."

"And that's unusual?" I ventured.

"Duh! He's always run around after her like a puppy who's lost his tail. I've seen Tasha let fly loads of times; she loses her temper, has a rant, and storms off. Zak follows, soothes her down, makes her sweet again. But not this time!"

"They weren't on good terms even before we went to the beach yesterday." I felt a bit guilty repeating something I'd overheard accidentally but it was obvious Millie wanted a good, girlie heart-to-heart. "She was sounding off because she thought Zak was supporting his family and the business rather than her. She said he was on their side, not hers."

"What did *he* say?" Millie was agog.

"That it wasn't a question of sides, something about the coast ride being important to them and he couldn't argue with neighbors without proof. He told her she was obsessed with hating Ray Grant and was trying to start a feud."

"Phew! And yet she still came out on the beach ride with us—how come?"

"Tasha wanted to take off but Zak got really harsh and told her she had to do the ride because it was part of her job. I gathered she doesn't just help out on a casual basis; she does it to earn money during college holidays. Oh yeah, and then Zak said she was always fighting with someone and she ought to get over it."

"I'm surprised she didn't brain him," Millie whistled.

"Well, you've practically got the whole story there but I'll spell it out anyway. Zak only started talking to me because he feels guilty about our ride being messed up. Once he said that I sort of coaxed the rest out of him."

"At least he *meant* to tell you," I said. "It was unintentional, but I was eavesdropping when I heard, wasn't I?"

"Whatever—don't beat yourself up about it. The whole thing hinges around the fact that Beacon Lodge is doing really well and they're planning to expand, build more rooms on the house so they can take more guests, and they're going to put in more riding facilities. Like you heard, though, the beach ride is a big draw for people booking here so it was a bombshell recently when Ray Grant announced he owned the whole of the beach frontage in the bay and was going to fence it all. Mr. Grant had uncovered some old deeds that show the true boundary of his land and said closing it off was necessary in order to stop trespassing on his private beach."

"Including everyone at Beacon Lodge?" I frowned at the thought of losing that great cove to swim in.

"He acknowledged the effect it would have on the holiday business so after a lot of negotiating he agreed to allow access across the edge of his land, though he's charging Val and Ed an annual fee for the privilege."

"Oh, that's what Tasha meant when she yelled at Mr. Grant about paying for her swim," I remembered. "It *does* seem pretty harsh. Anyway her objection is that she doesn't believe he's telling the truth about the boundary, does she?"

"Yeah, exactly, and she's totally out of order in my opinion." Millie had made her mind up. "I mean, the guy's got legal papers and everything."

"Well, Tasha obviously doesn't believe that." I was trying to be fair. "In which case I can kind of understand her getting so mad—"

"You're the only one who can! Val and Ed are furious at the way she's stirring things up They're afraid Ray Grant will retract his permission and include Beacon Lodge in his lockout. That would mean no beach rides for us!"

"I wouldn't want that," I admitted. "What does Zak think? He told his girlfriend he had to agree with his parents, but what does he *really* think?"

"He thinks she should butt out. He's sick of Tasha's fighting, and I'm pretty sure he's going to dump her."

"Right. And you're pleased about that." I was determined not to show any emotion myself.

"I'm thrilled skinny! Oh, you don't get it, Caitlin, you're so cool and detached you don't know what it's like to feel the way I do about Zak!"

"I'll try to imagine," I said drily.

"It's all right for you anyway. You've got a boyfriend all ready and waiting."

"Me?" I nearly fell over with shock. "Are you nuts? I don't have *any* friends at home, let alone a waiting list!"

"You've got Tom. He's dead keen, has been right from the start."

"Rubbish, we're just mates, that's all."

"You only have to snap your fingers and he'd come running. Zak wouldn't do that for me even if I tattooed a sign on my head."

"He likes you a lot." I wanted to cheer her up even though my own insides were bouncing around with joy at the thought of Zak being single. "He's always talking to you. Corinne was moaning about it only this morning."

"Corinne just wants to be the center of attention. Have

you *seen* the way she flirts with him? Mind you, she flirts with everyone."

"Meow." I thought I'd try lightening it up with some teasing. "Now you're just being catty. Corinne's all right."

"Hm," Millie said darkly. "Wait till she hears Zak and Tasha have split up. I bet she starts fluttering her eyelashes and slapping on the makeup even more."

"Poor Corinne." I ran my hand lightly along my pony's back. "She looked a real mess after she fell in, didn't she?"

"Like the Bride of Frankenstein!" Millie giggled. "But I s'pose at least she didn't go kicking off and making a huge fuss like someone else I know."

"I'm getting bored with the subject of Tasha and her temper." I gave her a good-natured shove. "Change the subject, why don't you?"

"Oh, all right. Hey there's what's-his-name—Paul." She waved in the direction of the house, and I saw the tall figure pause and raise a hand in response.

"Tom and I saw him last night. He said he was starting work here today." I didn't mention how we'd nearly run him over, knowing she'd probably tell her beloved Zak all about it. "I wonder what it is he's doing."

Millie knew, of course. "Clearing some land where the new extension will go. He's not a builder, Zak says, just a sort of local handyman."

"He goes fishing as well." I thought I might know something she didn't, but no chance.

"Yeah. His boat's called the *Sea Horse*. Nice name, isn't it?"

"Are you two still yakking?" Tom and Jacob were riding toward us. "We're supposed to be improving our riding skills while we're here, not strengthening our jaw muscles!"

"Ha ha, you're such a comedian," Millie returned equably. "Where are you going now, then?"

"There's a lunchtime picnic on the beach," Tom said solemnly. "But we told Val you two probably wouldn't be interested in coming along."

"As if." I knew he was teasing again. "Who else is going?"

"Everyone. Well, not Val because she's off somewhere, but all the guests plus Ed and Zak."

"If Zak's going Millie definitely won't want to join in." I was getting pretty good at joining in with the banter, I thought.

"I think I'd better." She was completely straight-faced. "I mean, I'll have to hang on to Fenton and Jade while their owners hold hands and gaze into each other's eyes, won't I?"

I saw an embarrassed flush creep over poor Tom's face and said quickly, "Look, Jacob, Millie's hair's on fire, better put it out quick!"

Catching on immediately, he obligingly poured the contents of his water bottle all over her head, leaving her spluttering and gasping.

By the time I'd dried her off and stopped her bashing Jacob and me, Tom's color had returned to normal. As we returned, still laughing, to the yard we saw Zak, looking as though a big black cloud was hovering directly over his head. He was obviously fretting over Tasha, I thought, and, feeling the incredible tingle the sight of him always gave me, I wondered just why life had to be so very, very confusing.

Chapter Eight

There wasn't much point in worrying about it so I just got on with enjoying the day, which was looking really promising. We put the horses in their stalls so they could rest in the cool while everyone sorted out their swimming gear and Ed and Zak filled backpacks with picnic food. Corinne, when she arrived back in the yard, was triumphantly waving a rubbery pink hat.

"Look what Val lent me! It's a swimming cap so if Teddy throws me in the water again it won't ruin my hair. What d'you think, Zak—cute, eh?"

He gave her a halfhearted smile and said, "I'm sure you'll look gorgeous in it."

Corinne batted her eyelashes so hard you could feel the

breeze they set up.

She was treated to one of Millie's finest dirty looks. "See what I mean," she muttered. "It's started! Zak hasn't even officially dumped Tasha yet and Corinne's already trying to muscle in."

"Put your claws away, Cat Woman," I said peaceably. "We're just going out for a nice picnic ride and swim. Don't give Zak any trouble, he looks weighed down already."

It was true. Zak seemed thoroughly miserable, and I wanted to tell him he'd be fine, he was *so* much better off without his tempestuous girlfriend.

"What are you daydreaming about?" Tom was stuffing towels in his backpack. "I've spoken to you twice, you were miles away."

"Who, me? Just—er—looking forward to the beach and hoping Jade will swim like she did yesterday."

"Sure she will, but you'd better hurry up—everyone else is ready."

They'd all led their horses out. Millie was already mounted and moving purposefully toward Zak. "I'll stay at the back with you, shall I?" she said ever-so-casually. "I expect Ed is leading today and—um—Chas prefers it when he's not in front."

"Okay." Zak sounded disinterested, but he swung into the saddle and kept Jet next to Millie's chestnut horse.

I gave an inward sigh I wasn't going to be near him and an outward smile at Tom. "Is it all right if I ride with you?"

"Oh sure." He looked delighted.

"Where's my dad?" Zak called across to Andy, who was nearest the gate. "Can you see him coming?"

"No." Andy peered toward the house. "Oh yeah, here he is, but—"

Ed arrived, rushing and breathless. "Sorry, very sorry about this but Val's just phoned and I have to take something into town for her straightaway."

"What about the beach?" Zak looked surly. "There should be two of us with the guests—"

"Oh, don't cancel the ride please!" Jacob spoke for all of us. "We're really looking forward to it."

"You can manage." Ed looked impatiently at his son. "You lead, this lot are sensible enough to stay behind you and keep out of trouble."

"Lovely." Corinne smiled sweetly. "I'll ride next to you then, Zak, seeing as Millie's horse likes to be at the back."

He shrugged and started moving away, not bothering to speak to his father, who turned and ran back to the house.

"Wonder what's so important?" I raised my eyebrows.

"Who cares?" Millie said gloomily. "All I know is it means that flirty witch has pinched my place now!"

"Don't worry." I couldn't help laughing at her disgruntled expression. "Zak's not in the best of moods anyway. You can keep me and Tom company as long as you don't make any more cracks about him and me."

She and Chas came over with me to join Tom, and the three horses moved on amicably together. Jacob and Andy were ahead of us while Corinne, chatting vivaciously, rode Teddy as close as she could to Zak and Jet. We stayed like that until we reached the gate in the long line of the Grants' fence.

"We'll stay in single file and keep fairly quiet through here if you don't mind." Zak's face was creased with anxiety. "I don't want to give the landowner any reason to complain today."

We obligingly did as he said, although it felt weird to be creeping silently on our way to what was supposed to be simply a few happy holiday hours on the coast. My spirits rose the minute we touched the beach, though. The cove lay before us, serene and beautiful under a clear blue sky. Jade, seeing that amazing stretch of ocean, whinnied and pranced with anticipation.

"She's keen," Millie remarked. "Oh, look at Corinne, you'd think she'd glued Teddy to Zak's leg, she's so close to him."

"She's probably worrying about her horse playing up again," Tom said patiently.

"You think?" Millie pulled a gruesome face and I laughed, too excited about swimming again to join in with getting jealous over Zak.

We did a similar routine to the day before, riding the horses along the sand and gradually getting closer to the waves. Blaze showed little sign of reluctance this time but Teddy was worse, refusing to even get his feet wet.

"I'm going to spend a little time with Corinne, helping her build her pony's confidence," Zak told us as we peeled off clothes and saddles. "I'll be keeping an eye on the rest of you, obviously, but as you only have the one instructor today I want you to be extra careful. Don't go too deep or too near Tiber Cliffs, don't fool around too much, and if anyone falls off or lets go of their horse the rest of you try to catch him. Okay?"

I couldn't wait but Millie was building up a major sulk, annoyed that her beloved Zak would be staying close to Corinne.

"Get real." Tom was fed up with her. "And get in the water—look, Caitlin's already swimming."

"Come on, Millie!" I waved ecstatically as Jade surged powerfully through the waves.

Jacob was next to join me, followed quickly by Andy.

"Wow! Get a load of Blaze!"

His chestnut horse was already enjoying himself, despite his action being slightly choppy and his nose pointing skyward. Jade looked like some kind of mystical marine creature in comparison, her outline sleek and streamlined as she swam effortlessly in line with the shore.

"Don't go too far that way." Jacob wasn't far behind on the strongly swimming Lucas. "There are dangerous cliff falls, remember."

"Yeah, I know." I just loved the feel of silky water moving against my legs. "We'll turn in plenty of time."

We met Tom on the return trip and tried to slow our pace so he could keep up.

"You're so fast." He was almost comically astounded. "I can just about stay in touch on dry land, but in the sea Jade covers twice the distance Fenton can manage."

"Lucas is really good too." I grinned over at Jacob.

"Yeah, it feels great to be one of the best at something." He patted his horse's gleaming wet neck.

"Where's Millie?" I squinted into the sun. "Oh, there she is."

"She and Andy are staying fairly near the shore in case Corinne manages to get Teddy in." Tom was getting left behind again. "At least, Andy's waiting for Corinne and—"

"And Millie's waiting for Zak," I finished his sentence

for him, and we both laughed.

It was totally, absolutely fabulous gliding through the ocean and I felt Jade and I could happily stay out here forever. On shore, Corinne was still struggling. With Zak's patient help and advice she was now riding Teddy through the shallows; the bay horse seemed to be enjoying the sensation of splashing in the gently lapping waves. Tom, Jacob, and I were swimming alongside our ponies, and I was showing off a bit by letting go of Jade and getting her to follow my every movement. She's been doing this on land for years and I was thrilled that, despite the excitement of tackling a completely new element, she still wanted to stay close by my side.

"Look," Tom called to me. "Corinne's nearly made it!"

I looked shoreward just as Teddy took a hesitant step that would take him across the coastal shelf and into deep water. Corinne seemed to be doing everything right—but again, at the very last minute Teddy chickened out, slamming on the brakes and twisting back into the shallows. She did really well to stay on his wet, slippery back but, slithering sideways, she lost the grip on her reins and grabbed a handful of mane instead. Teddy took off, thundering through the surf and along the beach with Zak, ever watchful, chasing close behind.

"She did that on purpose!" Millie was outraged. "Just to get Zak's attention."

"Don't be stupid," Andy growled. "She was doing her best, it's not her fault."

Millie then called Corinne a very rude word and an irritated Andy moved Blaze away from her, swimming out to join the three of us in deeper water.

Zak, meanwhile, had easily caught up with Teddy and was leading him back along the beach, deep in conversation with Corinne.

"Yah! Now she's doing her 'poor little helpless girl' act!" Millie really was in a vile temper. "Hogging all the attention—I'll fix her!"

We were too far away to stop her and watched in fascinated horror as she screamed loudly, "Oh stop it, Chas, stop it!" while waving her arms about and pretending to lose her balance. "Help! Help!"

Zak's head came up immediately as he turned away

from Corinne to look out to sea. With a mighty splash Millie hit the water and Chas, thoroughly alarmed, kicked out in panic, surging away from the shore.

"We'd better catch him." Tom hauled himself onto Fenton and I did the same, sliding easily onto Jade's back and turning her to cut across Chas's path.

Jacob was fast too, but it took a while before we managed to herd the panicky chestnut till I was close enough to grab his reins and bring him alongside. Being close to the other horses quickly calmed him, and we talked to him quietly, soothing his shattered nerves.

"Where's Tom?" I asked Jacob as I squinted into the sun.

"He and Andy have gone back to the shore, there they are—oh hey, something's going on!"

The direct glare of the sun made it difficult to see, but we could make out a sinister tableau on the beach. Tom was stood a little apart, holding Jet and Fenton, while Andy and Corinne huddled together, looking down at a figure stretched out on the sand. Kneeling beside it we could see Zak, bending and rising, his dark head lowering then turning away.

"He's giving mouth-to-mouth resuscitation—oh my God, that's Millie lying there!" Jacob's voice rose to a squeak.

For one stupid moment the thought flashed through my brain—*ooh that Millie, what she wouldn't do to get a kiss from Zak*—but then reality kicked in. This was an emergency; my friend was obviously unconscious and could well be in real danger.

"Oh no, Millie!" I nearly choked on rising tears and had to concentrate fiercely on keeping a grip on both Jade's and Chas's reins.

We surged out of the water and rushed over to the group. Just as we reached Tom, Millie gave a convulsive gasp and coughed out a stream of seawater, retching and twisting sideways, her face chalk white and ghastly. Zak sat back on his heels, his shoulders slumped with exhausted relief.

"Wh—what happened?" I knelt beside her.

She rubbed her head gingerly, her shoulders still heaving. "I got a kick from Chas when he took off. Not his fault, my fault, my fault."

"Don't blame yourself." Obviously no one had told Zak how Millie had landed in the sea. "If I'd been closer you'd have been all right. It took me so long to reach you, I thought—I thought—"

He looked so deeply upset my heart went out to him.

"She's fine, Zak, she's absolutely fine." I gave Millie a hug. "There's a lump on her head but—"

"It shouldn't have happened. Not the accident, the fact there was no one close by to rescue her. There should always be two of us, there should always—"

"Oi," Millie said weakly. "You heard my mate here, everything's fine. I'm so stupid the occasional kick in the head can only do me good!"

He tried to smile but still looked horribly shaken.

Corinne had fetched towels and now wrapped one quite tenderly around Millie's shoulders.

"Don't be kind to me, I don't deserve it." Millie was still shivering. "Look, everyone, I meant it when I said it was my fault. I pretended to fall off, but getting a hoof in the face wasn't actually in the plan!"

"Another reason for always having someone standing by." Zak dried himself listlessly. "People *do* fool around in the water, it happens all the time. We've had umpteen soakings but never anything as bad as this."

We spent quite a while drying ourselves and the horses as the sun beat down and the sea innocently lapped and sparkled on the shore. I made a thorough job of toweling and checking Chas over while gradually the color returned to Millie's face until she announced she was now quite hungry and we could all stop treating her so nicely.

"Yell at me," she told Zak. "It would make me feel better."

"I feel like yelling," he admitted gravely. "But not at you."

We then settled down to our picnic, and really it seemed that everyone was now enjoying themselves after our fright. Everyone except Zak, who, sitting a little detached from the rest of us, munched his way silently through a couple of sandwiches.

Millie, true to form, was soon cracking jokes.

"Trust me to head-butt my horse's hoof on the way

down." She touched the bruise gingerly.

"And trust you to be unconscious during your first kiss with Zak." I thought being facetious about the incident would help reduce its horror element. "How *was* it for you?"

"Oh don't." She hung her head. "What a total idiot I've turned out to be!"

"*You're* all right." I gave her a gentle hug. "Like Zak says, it was just a prank that went wrong."

"I wouldn't want to be in Ed's shoes when we get back, though." Tom lowered his voice. "Zak was adamant about needing someone with him and he's been proved right."

"I think it'll be Tasha who gets into trouble." Corinne tossed her head. "*She's* the one who didn't turn up today."

Zak insisted we take the ride back to Beacon Lodge at a very steady pace. He rode close beside Millie, even through the single-file stretch across Ray Grant's land, and checked how she was feeling every few minutes.

"Honestly, Caitlin, it was awful," Millie confided in me as I escorted her back to the house.

"I would have thought you'd lap it up," I teased her.

"Zak's undivided attention—isn't that exactly what you wanted?"

"Yeah, but not like this. I feel dead guilty, he looks worried sick, and it's totally my fault."

"He's already put you straight on that so stop giving yourself a hard time about it. Look on the bright side—he's probably so mad at Tasha he'll definitely dump her now."

"Yeah, and I even feel bad about that." She sighed again.

"Hi you two." We'd reached the kitchen and Val looked up, giving us a strained but still-sweet smile. "How did the picnic go?"

"Um—there was a bit of an accident." I gently smoothed Millie's hair back from her forehead to show the bruise.

"Oh dear." Val bustled into action, sitting Millie down and fetching a first-aid kit. "How did that happen?"

"I was being stupid, mucking about in the water," Millie said, looking deeply embarrassed again. "I—er—pretended to fall off and it panicked Chas, who accidentally gave me a bit of a kick."

Val's lips twitched as she dabbed stuff on the bruise. "That probably wasn't as funny as it sounds, but it's just a bump, I think you'll live."

"Bad choice of phrase, Mother." Zak, his face dark with anger, stood in the doorway. "There was nothing comical about it—Millie could have died. That's right, you heard—*she could have died!*"

Chapter Nine

Val gave a gasp, the color draining out of her face, and Millie said swiftly, "I'm all right, honestly, and it was totally my own fault anyway."

"There should have been two of us." Zak was beginning to sound like an overplayed CD. "I was too far away to reach her quickly. The kick knocked her out, and she was under the water a long time. She could have—"

"Yes, you said." Val pressed white lips together. "I'd better call a doctor and get you checked out properly, Millie."

"No way!" she cried. "Tell her, Caitlin, tell her I'm fine."

"She seems perfectly okay, ate her lunch and everything," I said.

"It's not the point," Zak was still fuming. "She could—"

"What's going on?" Ed made an appearance. "I've just

been to the stable yard. They're talking about an accident, Zak."

"Zak, go with your dad and tell him exactly what happened." Val took charge. "Millie, you're to come up to your room with me. I'm calling a doctor."

"No—but—I don't want—" My friend's voice faded as she was firmly ushered from the room.

"Upstairs in the office, Zak." Ed was looking grim. "Excuse us, Caitlin, while we get this sorted out."

I nodded dumbly and stood in the empty kitchen for a minute before making my way back to the yard. Here everything was nice and normal, everyone busy and happy, chatting and laughing as they washed seawater off the horses.

"I've done your girl." Tom was just starting on Fenton. "And Jacob's hosed Chas, so—hey what's the matter?"

"Nothing," I said slowly. "Well, nothing except I think World War Three has just broken out in the house."

"You look a bit shell-shocked." He lowered his voice. "I know you don't like fights, but don't let it get to you. Millie's accident was just that—an accident—so if the family want fight between themselves about it—"

"It's more than that." I swept a sponge across Fenton's back. "I think this whole 'Tasha versus Ray Grant' situation has gotten to them. Val was genuinely upset about Millie, though—she's sent for a doctor to check her over."

"That probably makes sense. You don't need to worry about your little friend, you know. She's as tough as they come."

"I just want everything to be—to be *nice*," I said. "This is such a great place and it's being spoiled for everybody."

"Like I said, none of it is our problem. Let's just enjoy our holiday and let the Meadows family get on with sorting out their troubles."

I knew he was right but I couldn't help worrying that Zak was now so mad he was at the point of quitting. As usual I seemed to have gotten it completely wrong. We were due some games practice later, before having another short jumping session with Ed, and to my great relief Zak was already in the field waiting for us. Keeping him company, with a grin as wide as the ocean, was Millie.

"Chas and I have been told to take the rest of the day

off," she told me importantly. "No riding for me, so I volunteered to be Zak's assistant instead."

"There's a surprise! How are you feeling?" I couldn't help smiling at her obvious delight.

"Great. Fine. Oh but—" She lowered her voice conspiratorially. "—I might occasionally feel faint if Zak forgets to pay me attention!"

"You're a shocker." I laughed and went to join the others for our warm-up.

"We're not going to compete today." Zak seemed to have recovered his normal good temper. "There will be a mini show later in the week for you to test your skills, but for now I want you honing some of the techniques needed."

He got us doing some exercises while riding, bending to touch our toes, standing in the stirrups and stretching, plus dismounting on the move.

"Stating the obvious, make sure you land facing forward and start running the moment your feet touch the ground." Zak got us riding in a wide circle while he and Millie stood in its center. "I'd like to see you do this on alternate sides—something your pony may not be used to, but it can prove invaluable in competition."

At one point he walked over to Corinne and adjusted the angle of her lower leg, but in the main he stayed close to Millie and *she* never stopped smiling.

The exercises were a big help, and when we also went over the vaulting technique I'd learned the day before I was pleased to see the improvement Jade and I had already made. Tom told everyone about my "loose schooling" demonstration—the way I'd taken my pony along the line of bending poles—and Zak immediately wanted to see us perform. Feeling pretty self-conscious I did it again, with Jade, bless her, cooperating beautifully.

"If I let go of Lucas's reins like that he'd just drop his head and eat." Jacob was impressed.

"And Blaze would freak out completely." Andy couldn't believe it. "You're not even touching your pony, it's all voice control."

"That's right." I was embarrassed at being the center of attention but very proud of Jade. "If I run in and out of the poles she'll follow me, but she's happy to do it this way too."

"It's amazing." Zak was the most animated he'd been all day. "You two will be unbeatable once you've learned how it's all done!"

I thoroughly enjoyed the afternoon training session, and when we moved on to the schooling ring I was thrilled to find our show jumping was also continuing to improve. As usual I spent much longer in my pony's stable than anyone else and was still happily sharing a cuddle with her when I became aware of voices in the yard.

"So you don't want me to tell her what's going on?" It was Zak's voice.

"Tasha's so hotheaded we'd prefer her not to know anything," Ed replied. "We do feel guilty about shutting her out but we can't risk her blurting out what we're doing. I still think Ray Grant is perfectly honest—tough and a bit ruthless, but if he's legally entitled to that land then that's it as far as I'm concerned."

"But Mum's not so sure?"

"Well, she didn't believe Tasha at first, thought she was doing her usual drama-queen act, but the rumors about the guy are worrying, and she's decided to investigate his claim a bit further." Ed sighed. "It's already been a long process and your mother wants it kept quiet because she doesn't want things jeopardized by one of your girlfriend's outburst in front of the guests. They should be thinking about enjoying their holiday and taking in new training ideas—we don't want them concerned with our problems."

This put me in an awkward situation—did I now pop my head over the door and say, *I'm still here and I heard what you said*, or did I stay put and stay quiet? I chose the line of least confrontation and kept very still.

"They're a nice bunch of kids," Ed continued. "And deserve better attention but with a bit of juggling we'll make sure they get all the riding they want."

"Yeah, you're right. I've just got to find a way of telling Tasha the beach trips are still on."

"Absolutely, as long as she's not involved in taking them. Val says we can't risk upsetting Ray Grant again." Their voices faded as they moved away, and when I finally looked out the yard was empty.

"Honestly, you'd think wanting to spend as much time as I can with you couldn't possibly get me into trouble, but it seems to be turning me into some sort of spy!" I kissed Jade's nose fondly. "Still, at least I overheard good stuff about the riding this time."

She nudged me as if in agreement, and we both stepped out of her stable for the short walk to the field. Fenton was quite near the gate and greeted her ecstatically, practically ushering her across the grass to their favorite rolling spot. I watched for a while till they both settled down and returned, feeling content and happy, to the house. Tom was hovering in the boot room, his face breaking into a smile as soon as I appeared.

"I was just coming to look for you, Caitlin. Everything okay?"

"Everything's brilliant." I kicked my boots off. "I was just spending some time with my Very Best Friend."

"But Millie's in the—oh, you mean Jade, don't you?"

"I do." I grinned at him, glad I never felt shy or awkward in his company. "She always treats me better than the human variety."

"That's nice." He gave me a sidelong glance. "But some of us two-legged friends think you're pretty cool too, you know."

I thought it was sweet of him to say so but soon found myself in the sort of muddle I seemed to get myself into when it comes to people. Millie was almost hyper with excitement: Having spent most of the afternoon as Zak's "assistant," she'd convinced herself there was a future for the arrangement.

"Zak's so *lovely*," she sighed. "And he seems totally over his sulk about Tasha. I think his parents made him realize he's better off without her."

I very nearly told her what I'd overheard. Zak hadn't sounded like someone who'd happily dumped his girlfriend—in fact he'd been planning the best way of keeping her away from the beach, but firmly in his life. The snatch of conversation I'd heard about the boring land boundary wasn't conclusive, though, so I decided not to burst Millie's bubble and tell her I thought Tasha was still very much in the picture. She'd soon find out anyway, I figured, so why get involved? The next morning, cross-country with Val was on the program, but Ed told us as we were saddling up that some rescheduling was necessary.

"My wife has to go out on urgent business again," he apologized. "But I promise anyone who wants it will get their training session later in the day. Meanwhile you can choose between show jumping or mounted games practice, with Val offering dressage tomorrow."

"What about a beach ride?" Jacob loved the swimming as much as I did.

"Er—yes, Zak and I will be escorting a group to the cove for anyone who'd like another picnic."

"Count us all in then." Andy sounded enthusiastic. "Oh sorry, Corinne, would you prefer not?"

"No, I *want* to get Teddy in the ocean." The blond girl sounded determined. "He nearly made it yesterday till—"

"Till I made a total dork of myself," Millie finished cheerfully. "Don't worry, everyone—I learned my lesson and I think Chas deserves a nice peaceful swim to restore his confidence so I'm up for it too."

"That's settled then." Ed started spreading the sack mats on the ground.

"I'll do that for you." We hadn't heard Tasha's quiet arrival. "If you want me to, that is."

"Of course I do." Ed's smile of greeting was slightly wary, but Zak's delight at seeing her shone out of every pore.

Tasha was on her best behavior, being helpful and sunny with everyone and a real asset to Zak's teaching.

"It's not fair." Poor Millie was sunk in gloom. "As soon as she turns on the charm Zak goes to pieces. He's looking at her like she's the best thing since plasma TV and totally forgiven her for yesterday."

"Oh well." I was pretty depressed at the gorgeous redhead's reappearance too, but didn't admit it. "It probably won't last—that temper of hers is bound to erupt sooner or later."

On that score I was proved right a lot quicker than I'd imagined. We had a brilliant games session—hard work but really good fun. After eight games the score was even, both teams winning four each.

"What shall we do for a decider this time, Tasha?" Zak looked at her lovingly.

"The bride-and-groom race was a bit of a hit." She smiled flirtatiously back at him. "But we could give it a bit of a twist. This time the girls have to rescue the boys."

"Great idea," Zak said. I saw a gleam appear in Millie's eyes at the thought of Zak seated behind her with his arms wrapped around her waist.

I knew that was what was going through her mind because I was looking forward to exactly the same thing! The guys all dismounted and hitched their horses to the fence. Just as they set off for the pickup point, Ed strolled over to watch.

"Val's about to leave," he told us. "So I thought I'd come over and cheer on the final now that I've got the picnic all ready."

"Picnic?" Tasha, on Sabrina, was only a few feet from me. Jade and I clearly heard the sharp intake of breath she took.

"Er—yes, didn't Zak tell you?" Ed looked at his son's retreating back. "He and I are taking the guests to the beach."

"Where? To the cove?" Tasha's voice rose higher. "Across Ray Grant's so-called land?"

"I thought you understood the situation," Ed said

stiffly. "If not, I'll discuss it later."

"You'll discuss it now!" She turned on him like a flame-haired tiger. "I assumed you realized I only came back on the understanding we no longer pander to Ray Grant's illegal demands."

"And I assumed you understood we still use the route but *you* are not to be involved. Val's apologized to Ray Grant for your tirade and—"

"She's done what?" Tasha screamed. Zak spun round and stared at them both in horror. "How can you humiliate me like this, getting Val to say sorry? I—I—oh, wait till I get my hands on her!"

She spun Sabrina and began galloping across the field.

Zak, running desperately, yelled, "Caitlin, go with her! Don't let her reach the house!"

Yeah, I know what you're thinking. Me, with my hatred of confrontation, rows, and all highly charged emotional situations, being instructed to get involved! It must have been an instinctive reaction to the passion in Zak's voice because I found myself touching Jade's sides to perform a perfect forehand turn so I could race after the rapidly disappearing palomino. Jade's great speed meant we weren't far behind, arriving outside the front door of the house just as Tasha wrenched it open. She'd leapt off Sabrina and looped her reins over the fence so I dismounted rapidly, calling, "Wait for me, Jade, wait," as I followed. I could hear Tasha yelling Val's name as she ran upstairs and, although I had no idea what I was going to *do* in this explosive situation, I kept racing after her. I reached the broad landing at the top of the stairs and looked round wildly. For a few seconds I had no idea where she'd gone till I heard her swear loudly.

"Tasha!" I called, my voice slightly trembly.

She came stalking out of the door to my right, the room used as an office by Ed and Val.

"She's not there, she's already left." She sounded defeated. "I needed to ask why they're treating me like this. It's *their* fight I'm fighting!"

"Come on." I hooked my arm through hers (pretty bravely I thought) and led her back down the stairs. "Zak will here any minute."

He arrived just as we stepped outside, skidding to a halt

on his black horse.

"Caitlin, thank you, you got her." He vaulted over the fence and ran toward us.

"Oh, I see." Tasha's eyes narrowed dangerously. "You sent Caitlin to stop me getting to your mother. You're still on their side, aren't you, Zak?"

"Don't start. I've told you it's not about taking sides."

"Of course it is." She wrenched her arm free. "And the stupid thing is I'm on *your* side, you and your parents. It's because of you I'm battling Ray Grant and his arrogant fence and his private beach!"

"I know." Zak moved warily closer. "But you're going about it the wrong way."

"The wrong—how can your way be the right one? Paying that man to ride across land that isn't his?"

"We don't have any proof of that, and the business *needs* that beach ride."

"I should go," I interjected timidly. "Let you—um—sort it out between you."

"No!" To my surprise Tasha grabbed my arm and put it back through hers again. "I need you. There's another beach ride, Caitlin, I'll show it to you and then *you* can tell Ed and Val that it's fine to use that route instead of kowtowing to Ray Grant."

"You can't involve Caitlin, she's a guest!" Zak ran his hands through his hair in frustration. "We're doing our best to keep the problem private and not spoil these kids' holiday."

"Just one ride, that's all." Tasha was practically begging. "Please, Caitlin. It doesn't mean you have to get involved in any row. I think there's a real alternative to using the cove and if, as a guest, you could just check it out—"

She sounded so passionate, so persuasive that I found myself nodding reluctantly. "I'll take a look but I don't think my opinion's going to influence anybody."

"It will. You're easily the best person I could ask, you're so sensible and levelheaded."

"Er—thanks." I looked at Zak. "What do you think?"

"If you don't mind, it wouldn't hurt to try." He shrugged apologetically. "And it'll give Tasha time to cool down a bit."

I felt her twitch angrily but with an obvious effort she

stayed calm. We walked over to the fence where the three horses were waiting.

"Look at that." Zak pointed. "Jade isn't tied up."

"No, I asked her to wait," I said simply. He shook his head in amazement.

Tasha, still fired up, was already climbing into Sabrina's saddle.

"Do we need to tell Ed where we're going?" I ventured.

"No." Zak looked across the field. "He's already taken the group off for jumping schooling so we won't bother him."

And you won't risk Tasha sounding off again, I thought as we left the field and started moving along the drive.

The first part of the ride was the same as before, turning left to follow the track through the copse. Instead of following the line of new fencing around the Grants' grounds, though, Zak took a sharp left fork across some scrubby common land. Tasha, eager for me to approve the route, kept pointing out its benefits, and I thoroughly enjoyed the long, exciting canter along a broad track. As we slowed the pace I became aware of a sound in the distance.

"Is that traffic I can hear?" I asked.

Zak nodded. "We have to cross a busy road, I'm afraid."

"It doesn't take long, though," Tasha put in eagerly.

It must have been the main coastal route for cars, with several lanes of fast-moving vehicles thundering past. Luckily Jade is absolutely bombproof in traffic and didn't object to crossing to grass division, then waiting for a gap and crossing again.

"See!" Tasha looked across at her boyfriend. "That was fine—Caitlin had no problem with the road."

"Caitlin's pretty special." Zak had no idea his phrase made my insides vault about gymnastically. "But I think a lot of our guests and their horses would have trouble with it."

She sighed theatrically. "Well, if you're going to take that attitude—"

"I'm not." He didn't look at her. "Let's just do the ride and let Caitlin make up her own mind about it."

The next part of the route was pretty dull but perfectly safe, a long, narrow path, completely paved so we couldn't canter, ending at another road, this one lined with houses. It was quiet, with only an occasional car or lorry passing us, and as the number of houses thinned I could smell a salt tang on the wind.

"The sea's just ahead," Tasha pointed, and there it was, glinting and sparkling under the midmorning sun. This was a much bigger cove, bordered on our right by slate-gray cliffs forming a promontory, but stretching for what seemed miles to our left.

"It's beautiful," I said honestly. "But there are a lot of people around, aren't there?"

The beach, of fine golden sand, was liberally dotted with groups of holidaymakers sunbathing on loungers, resting under stripey shades, and splashing happily in the sea. The thought of a group of seven or eight horses galloping across the beach and surging through the waves among them was ludicrous. I knew immediately that Tasha's idea just wasn't going to work.

Chapter Ten

Tasha tried hard to persuade me. "It's crowded at this time of day because it's easy for people to drive here, but if we set off early in the morning or maybe late evening we should be able to get a swim."

"Yeah?" I said doubtfully. "It would have to be empty for us lot to take over the beach, wouldn't it?"

"Not necessarily," Tasha argued. "Sabrina and I have swum here when other people are around."

"When?" Zak challenged.

She lowered her eyes. "Well, not for a while."

"You came here *once* on a cloudy day when you thought it'd be quiet and you said it was a nightmare trying to avoid the tourists." Zak made her look at him and added gently, "It's not going to work, Tasha. Unless we get here at five in the morning it's always going to be crowded—that means no picnics, no freedom, no—"

"What happened to Caitlin making her own decision?" She sounded near to tears. "You're putting her off completely."

"He's only saying what I'm thinking," I said honestly. "This beach is like a different world compared with the cove. How come they're so unalike?"

"The cove is cut off by Tiber Cliffs," Zak explained. "There's no road access so even the locals don't bother with it much."

"And the few that do have been excluded completely by Ray Grant," Tasha said bitterly. "People could always walk or ride along the grassy track to get there, but since Ray has claimed it belongs to him he won't allow it. He's permitted Beacon Lodge access—at a price of course—but I'll bet anything you like he'll bar you as well when it suits him."

"I don't know about that, but in the meantime we *have* to comply with his restrictions." Zak turned to me, his gorgeous blue eyes filled with concern. "I'm sorry, Caitlin, you don't even know what we're talking about—"

"Yes, I do. Your neighbor's got papers that show he owns the whole beach frontage of the cove."

"Er—yes." The blue eyes widened. "But Tasha—"

"Doesn't believe him and thinks you should refuse to pay for the privilege of riding through there."

"You're smart." Tasha nodded approvingly. "See, Zak, the kids all know the score so your family might just as well oppose Ray Grant like I do."

"I—um." Zak must have been recalling his father's instructions not to discuss the neighbors with her, especially in front of someone like me. "Look, there's no point in staying here, we might as well turn round and go home."

"So you can be in time to help Ed with the picnic at the cove?" Tasha was starting to fume again and all the way back she kept niggling at Zak, trying to persuade him to veto the ride through Ray Grant's land.

He stayed very quiet, occasionally shaking his head at her persistence, but refusing to give way.

"You're supposed to be my boyfriend!" she yelled at one

point. "But you don't act like one. I can just about take your parents opposing everything I say but not you as well, Zak!"

"My family aren't against you—" he began, but she was whipping up a storm.

"Yes they are. They take everybody's word against mine—look how they believe Ray Grant and take no notice of what I told them about him!"

"It's not like that—" He tried again but she pushed past on Sabrina, walking her horse along Beacon Lodge's drive, her back stiff with anger and hurt.

I heard Zak mutter something testy under his breath before he smiled apologetically at me. "Don't worry, I won't let this spoil your riding. My parents will sort this out, but in a quiet, civilized way."

"It's fine." I wanted to reassure him, he looked so worried. "I—oh, there's your dad."

Ed had come to meet us, but *quiet and civilized* was not the way I'd describe his greeting.

"You've got a nerve!" He glared at Tasha, and there were practically sparks coming out of his eyes. "I've just spent half an hour trying to calm Ray Grant down after your latest crazy trick. Just what the heck is the *matter* with you?"

Tasha blinked. "With me? What am I supposed to have done?"

"Don't act the innocent with me." Ed took hold of Sabrina's bridle and led her round so Tasha was now facing back toward the gate. "Just get out and don't bother coming back this time!"

"Hang on, hang on!" Zak rode swiftly toward him. "What's this about?"

"Your girlfriend, in her hotheaded way, decided to take her fight with Ray to a new level. She's been over there and slung my sea horse through one of his windows!"

"He *saw* her do that? When?" Zak had gone pale.

"No, he didn't see, but who else is crazy enough to do something like that? The thing was in its place before I came over to watch you, then Tasha flies into one of her rages, goes and grabs it, then flings it at the Grant house."

"No she didn't." Zak leaned over and held Tasha's hand. "I've been with her every minute. You're wrong, Dad."

"Who else then? That sea horse could only be taken by someone in the house, and who else except Tasha would sneak it out and use it in an act of pure vandalism?"

"You always have to blame her!" Zak was losing the temper he held so carefully in check. "Tasha's right—whatever happens you think only the worst of her. Because Ray Grant told you she was the guilty party you took his word for it when it's probably just one more lie he's invented."

"He can't *invent* a great lump of glass with a sea horse in it." Ed's temper matched his son's. "He heard a crash and there it was, lying in a pile of shattered window on his living room floor! He knew whose it was, of course, and brought it straight here to show me. There's no doubt about that, Zak, so who do you suggest stole it—one of the guests? They're the only people, apart from us, who had access to it."

"Yeah, all right then, maybe it *was* one of them," Zak shouted, making Jet twitch and stamp his feet.

"Why? What possible quarrel can they have with Ray? It's only your girlfriend who's fighting him like an alley cat."

"Maybe someone did it knowing Tasha would get the blame."

"That makes sense." Tasha was nearly crying. "The girls want me off the scene so they can make a play for Zak, while the guys—"

"That's enough!" Ed thundered. "Don't you think you've done enough damage to our family's business without trying to implicate these nice kids? Zak, go and make sure they're all okay while I escort Tasha off my land."

"No!" Zak's chin was high. "Tasha didn't touch that stupid sea horse and she didn't smash Ray Grant's window with it. If you throw her out I go too!"

Keeping well away and trying to disappear into the background, I was, nevertheless, watching all three of them closely—and I saw, *definitely* saw, a guilty expression flash across Tasha's face.

She gripped her boyfriend's hand more tightly and looked directly at him. "Thank you. You don't know what that means to me, Zak."

Still fired up, the look he gave her in return was of pure

devotion.

I saw Ed's shoulders slump. "You'd both better go then," he said bitterly and turned on his heel to walk away.

I watched Zak and Tasha ride back down Beacon Lodge's drive, the black horse's sides almost touching the palomino's, until both horses and their riders disappeared from view. I felt shaky and upset and, as always, wanted a soothing chat with Jade. I took her back to her stable and she listened while I untacked and brushed her, nudging me in her gentle, comforting way.

"There you are!" Tom's head appeared at the door. "What are you two talking about?"

"Just discussing this morning's goings-on." I managed a smile. "Jade agrees with me—she doesn't think much of them."

"Phew, your horse is smart! She's right—it's more like a battle zone than a riding holiday! Where did you go after you chased Tasha?"

"We went for a ride," I said vaguely, not sure if I should tell him everything.

"Excellent choice for someone who doesn't like rows.

Twenty minutes after you disappeared all hell broke loose here."

"Oh?" I gave Jade a last cuddle and stepped outside to join him. "What happened?"

"We *were* going over to the school for some jumping," Tom said. "But Ed was real agitated—upset by the way Tasha had blown up. He asked if we minded taking a break till he'd sorted things, so everyone kind of wandered off. Millie was looking pretty shattered so I said I'd put Fenton in his box and join her back at the house. I was hoping you'd be there but—"

"Zak and Tasha asked me to go with them to another beach to check it out." I realized there was no point keeping anything secret.

"Right. Well, we hung around, not knowing where everyone was, when the doorbell rang—a great continuous burst like someone was leaning on it really hard."

"Ray Grant?" I guessed.

"Ed opened the door and the guy just burst in waving that hefty paperweight that's always on Ed's desk. You know the one—it's a sea horse inside a big—"

"Chunk of glass? I remember Zak showing it to me, but I didn't take much notice. It was thrown through one of Ray's windows, wasn't it?"

"That's right. Grant was going ballistic, shouting and swearing and waving this thing about. He was saying, 'She threw this sea horse of yours knowing I'd recognize it straightaway!' Ed tried to calm the guy but you could see he was badly rattled too. He took the paperweight and said, 'But it was on my desk this morning. I used it just before I went over to see the riders.'"

"Ed told us it must have been Tasha who threw it," I said slowly.

"Yeah, well, that's what Ray Grant was yelling."

"It couldn't be. She went into the house and ran upstairs to the office looking for Val but she didn't have time to reach the Grants' house. We were with her the whole time."

"Their front door isn't far from the end of the drive, you know," Tom said. "It's only a bit farther down the road on the opposite side. You can reach it in five minutes."

"Tasha didn't have five minutes."

"Well, maybe she gave it to someone else," he suggested.

"We didn't meet anyone. And anyway, where would she hide a big lump of glass? She had no bag and she was wearing a T-shirt and riding breeches. There was nowhere to stash anything bigger than a postage stamp."

"Oh." Tom thought about it. "That's going to disappoint Millie. She was devastated when Tasha showed up and within minutes had Zak running after her. Millie said straightaway it had to be Tasha because she could easily have nicked the sea horse from Ed's desk and who else would want to lob it through Ray Grant's window?"

"Tasha's got her own theory." I kept my voice expressionless. "She thinks it was probably one of the guests stirring up trouble in the hope of getting rid of her."

Tom let out a long whistle. "Is that what she thinks? Wait till Millie and Corinne hear her say that!"

"They won't get the chance." I hung Jade's saddle and bridle in the tack room. "Ed told her to get out but Zak was so furious he went with her."

"You're kidding!" He gaped at me.

I shook my head, trying to look unconcerned. "At least it means no more shouting matches, I suppose."

"Yeah, and not much riding either!" He opened the yard gate for me. "I told you Zak and Tasha did all the fun stuff last year. There's no way Val and Ed will be able to do as much."

"I guess that's an end to the beach rides then." I felt utterly depressed: No more swimming, no more Zak. "Millie will go mad."

We found my new friend in the dining room.

"Hungry?" Tom greeted her. "If so, bad news I'm afraid. It's only sandwiches in the kitchen today."

"I know, I saw Ed unpacking what should have been our picnic lunch." Millie sighed gloomily. "I'm only in here because I'm keeping an eye out for Zak. I saw him going down the drive with Tasha. My guess is Ed's thrown her out and Zak was making sure she went off the premises."

"Mm, you're half right." I swiftly told her what I knew.

"No!" she yelled, holding her hands over her ears to block out what she was hearing. "Zak wouldn't go with her after what she did!"

"She didn't do anything," I reminded her. "We don't just have Zak's word for that—I was with her too, and there's no way she could have slung that sea horse through the Grants' window."

"Oh come on, don't be nuts!" Millie was enraged. "She must have sneaked away when you weren't looking."

"No." I shook my head firmly.

She bounced over to me and stared intently into my face. "You're not one hundred percent sure, are you, Caitlin? I can see there's just a bit of doubt in your mind—oh tell me, please—it *has* to be Tasha and Zak *has* to come home."

I hesitated and this time Tom joined in. "Millie's right, there's something you're not telling us."

"It's nothing, it's just—well, I was watching Tasha's face and she looked guilty—only for a minute but it was there—she looked guilty."

"That's because she is," Millie crowed. "Go and tell Ed!"

"No." I was adamant. "I might have read her expression

wrong. What I saw isn't evidence, just an impression I got."

"Caitlin's right." Tom was thinking hard. "So the best thing we can do is try a bit of detective work—find out just who *did* have the opportunity."

"More or less everyone," Millie said instantly.

"But hang on." Something had occurred to me. "How would any of the guests know about the paperweight? Why didn't they just chuck a stone or something through the window?"

"Ed showed us all his beloved sea horse, didn't he, Tom?" Millie answered at once. "It wasn't long before you and Jade arrived, Caitlin. We were talking about swimming and Corinne prattled on about how good Teddy was going to be. She said something about wanting him to be a sea horse and Ed immediately went upstairs and brought the paperweight down to show us a real one. So everyone could have known it was the perfect thing to let Ray Grant think the damage was caused by someone from here. The question is *why* would they do it?"

"To set Tasha up?" I offered. "She and Zak thought one

of us lot might have done it hoping that she'd get the blame."

"Why do they think that?" Millie looked from Tom to me and back again.

"Er—" I said, too cowardly to tell her that Tasha knew about the crush most girls had on her boyfriend.

"She knows a lot of the guests would prefer it here without her," Tom said tactfully.

"Because she's a total pain?" Millie was blissfully unaware. "Yeah, that figures."

"Come on, let's get something to eat." I started walking to the kitchen. "And we could put your detective thing into practice, Tom, find out where everyone was when the sea horse was taken."

Corinne, Andy, and Jacob had already started on the picnic lunch, looking, I have to say, a bit fed up.

"It's not exactly what I imagined doing on this holiday." Corinne shook her sculpted curls petulantly. "Sitting round a kitchen table instead of on a beach."

"It can't be helped." Jacob was steadily plowing through a big plateful. "Ed will sort it out. I expect he and Zak will take us to the cove later."

"Duh! I don't think so!" Millie was all drama. "Zak isn't even going to be around and it's all Tasha's fault."

"Oi, cool it, you." I helped myself to some food. "We don't know that."

"We don't know much really." Tom's manner was, as ever, calm and pleasant. "It's all a bit of a mystery. We need to find out where everyone was between the time Tasha rowed with Ed and rode off and—oh, shall we say half an hour later?"

"Why?" Andy looked curiously at the three of us. "We heard a bit of a commotion earlier—is there trouble?"

"Yeah. Someone vandalized the neighbors' house."

"The Grant place?" Corinne raised her eyebrows. "I nearly rode in there earlier."

"Is that where you went?" Andy looked at her. "I saw you go down the Beacon Lodge drive but when I went to find you, you'd disappeared."

"When Ed canceled the jumping class I decided to take a few postcards and ride to the post box we passed on the way here," Corinne explained. "And I thought the turn I found was a shortcut but in fact it led to the Grants' house so I turned back to the road and saw you."

"I was going to do some work in the school," Andy told us. "But when I saw no one else was bothering I decided to follow Corinne instead."

"Do you want my alibi now?" Jacob reached for another packet of crisps. "That's what you're doing, isn't it—collecting alibis?"

"Er—we're just trying to sort out in our minds where everyone was." Tom looked slightly embarrassed his "detecting" had been sussed. "So yeah, we are asking for alibis I guess."

"Oh, whoops." Jacob pulled a face. "I don't have one. Does that mean I'm guilty of whatever horrible crime's been committed?"

"Shouldn't think so," Tom said, laughing. "Actually I was on my own for fifteen minutes and so was Millie, so none of us are in the clear."

"Except me," Corinne said instantly. "I told you where I was."

"But Ray Grant's house is the scene of the crime," Millie cried. "Tell them exactly what happened, Caitlin. You'll say it all cool and precise, not like me."

I went through the story of the paperweight through the window and how Ray Grant and Ed thought it must be Tasha's work.

"Of course it was." Corinne nodded vehemently. "Who else?"

Slightly wearily, I told her how I could vouch for Tasha's innocence.

"Excuse me." Val's voice cut in. "Would you mind going through that one more time, Caitlin?"

"Sure." I got up from my chair, blushing because she'd heard us discussing her family this way.

"Come up to the office, dear." She gave the sweet smile that looked more strained than ever. "I'm truly sorry to ask you but you obviously know the situation so—"

"It's fine." I followed her up the stairs.

I'd never been in Ed's office, which was a model of neatness and order. The walls were lined with shelves, each bearing dozens of books about horses; there were prints and photographs of horses everywhere and a big, solid desk with a leather top plus two shabby but comfortable-looking chairs.

"Sit down, Caitlin." Ed was slumped behind the desk, his back to the window. "I'm sorry—"

"You don't have to keep apologizing," I said swiftly. "I know you've got problems and if there's anything I can do to help, I will."

"Thank you." He gave me a tired, but genuine, smile. "You told me you have the gist of what's going on, so can I ask you exactly what happened when Zak sent you galloping after Tasha this morning?"

I told them both the story as succinctly as I could. When I stopped there was a brief and uneasy silence.

"So Tasha definitely didn't leave here with the paperweight?" He moved it to a central position on the desk. "Here it is, you see."

Now that I could study it properly I could see it was a quirky kind of object. An irregular, solid-looking piece of amber-colored glass, shaped and polished so it reflected the light streaming in through the window, it contained in its depths the perfect, charming form of a single sea horse.

"It's very nice," I said, somewhat lamely. "But Tasha couldn't have taken it. She had no pockets, nowhere to hide it. We left straightaway and both Zak and I were with her till we got back here and you—you—"

"Set on her." Ed groaned and put his head in his hands. "I'm sorry, Val. If you'd been here you'd have dealt with it so much better."

"Ray Grant upset you," she said loyally. "He assumed straightaway that Tasha had caused the damage and you—"

"Agreed with him. She was like a—a demon the way she flew at me earlier. When I told her you'd made Grant an apology I thought she was going to rip your head off."

"That's why Zak told me to stop her," I said helpfully. "So she wouldn't."

"That was very brave of you," Val said. "I've seen grown men tremble when Tasha's in a rage, but it seems as far as the vandalism is concerned we've done her an injustice."

"*I* have, you mean." Ed rose to his feet. "I'll have to go to her house and apologize, persuade Zak to return and—"

"Not yet," Val said firmly. I could clearly see who made the rules here. "Let them both cool down first."

"But I can't bear Zak turning against us." Ed was so upset he hardly noticed I was there. "You know how much he means to me. I want him here."

Unexpected tears prickled behind my eyes and at the back of my throat. My own dad had turned his back completely on me, to the extent of leaving the country to begin life abroad with his new family, and yet here was a father who couldn't bear a separation of only a few miles. I felt a burning hatred for Tasha, thinking about the guilty expression, which I was sure meant *she* was responsible for the gaping rift within this once united family.

Chapter Eleven

I left Val trying to cheer Ed up and walked slowly back to the kitchen, thinking hard. Tom was right, the only way to clear this up was to do some detective work, but instead of concentrating on the alibis and motives of the guests I needed to work out just *how* Tasha had managed to stage the sea horse stunt. Millie was waiting in the hallway to find out what was happening now.

"Is Zak coming home?" she asked eagerly. Her face fell when I shook my head. "I thought Ed would rush off and get him, you know, apologize to Tasha and bring them both back here."

"I thought you didn't want the girlfriend around," I said lightly.

"I don't, really, but it's not fair Tasha should be blamed for something she didn't do." Millie was very honest. "And I'd much rather have Zak around, even with Tasha, than not see him at all."

"Come on then." Tom came out to join us. "I've got a pen and some paper, let's go back in the dining room and make some notes."

"This is you in your role of Ace Detective, is it?" I grinned at him.

"Absolutely." He sat down at the table and wrote a heading in capital letters—OPPORTUNITY. "Okay." He paused. "We know the sea horse paperweight was definitely on Ed's desk this morning, so who had the chance to nip up and lift it in order to sling it through Ray Grant's window? Let's start with the people who couldn't—they are Ed himself, Val, Tasha, and—"

"Hang on." Millie was frowning. "You can't rule out Ed and Val. We don't know where either of them was when the window got smashed, and they could have taken it at any time. We only have Ed's word it was on his desk when he left the house."

Tom and I gaped at her.

"Um—well—yeah, but surely we know Ed's telling the truth, don't we? You saw him when Grant came bursting into the house—Ed was genuinely astounded."

"And Val had an appointment in town," I put in. "Anyway—*why* would they do such a thing? They're the ones who want to keep the peace with the neighbors at all costs."

"That's true," Millie conceded. "But I just wanted to point out that it's not just the guests who had—" She ran her fingers under Tom's headline, OPPORTUNITY.

"Thanks for complicating things even more," I grumbled. "I've just been with Val and Ed and they're both totally shattered by this. I, for one, completely believe Ed's version, so let's take it from there. Ed says the sea horse was in its place when Tasha and I ran into the house. She didn't take it and I didn't take it—and Zak didn't even go inside. We then rode to the beach and didn't return till after it was all over so I can't see how it can be any of us three."

I was hoping my fellow detectives would see a flaw in

my logic, a possible method that could explain how Tasha had managed to pinch the sea horse and use it without either Zak or me seeing her.

"That seems irrefutable." Tom pretended to go all pompous. "If Zak and Tasha had supplied alibis for each other I'd be suspicious, but the fact you were there, Caitlin, definitely proves they're both innocent."

"Yeah, you're right." Millie sighed deeply. "Shame, I'd love it to be Tasha! Oh well, let's see whose name can definitely go on the opportunity list."

"Mine for a start." He wrote TOM underneath the heading. "When Ed abandoned the jumps class I went to the yard on my own, settled Fenton down, got a hay net, all the usual stuff. I reckon I was on my own for about fifteen minutes—plenty of time."

"Okay, so you'd better put my name next," Millie said with a shrug. "I came straight back to the house and read a mag till you came in but I don't think anyone saw me."

"And you didn't hear anything—no one going upstairs, for instance?" I asked.

"Nope. I was in the kitchen at the back, didn't notice a

thing."

"Jacob said he just mooched about, had a ride round, didn't see anyone." Tom was busy scribbling it all down. "So he's another one who had the *opportunity* of paying the Grant house a visit."

"Agreed—he isn't in the clear either. Mind you, from where I'm standing Corinne looks like Suspect Number One, doesn't she?" Millie laughed unkindly. "*Her* alibi is that she was riding 'by accident' along Ray Grant's drive. Duh!"

"While Andy was also nearby, apparently, looking for her." I shook my head. "Don't you think if either of them *was* guilty they'd have come up with a better story?"

"It could be a double bluff," Millie said darkly.

Tom glared at her. "Don't make it any more difficult than it is! Okay, we have five main suspects, any of whom *could* have taken the sea horse and used it. Now it's the million-dollar question, isn't it? *Why* would Millie, Corinne, Andy, Jacob, or I *want* to do such a thing?"

Watching him write MOTIVE carefully on the next line, I said diffidently, "The obvious reason is to implicate

Tasha I guess."

"In which case at least four of us had a motive then." Millie cheerfully ticked them off on her fingers. "Corinne and me fancy Zak so want Tasha off the scene. Andy fancies Corinne so wants Zak off the scene. Jacob fancies Tasha but she ignored him so he wants revenge."

Tom and I stared at her.

"Er—right," he said weakly. "You don't have a motive for me then?"

"Can't think of one. The person you fancy—"

"You're making all this up," I interrupted quickly. "It's not for real—none of you lot would cause criminal damage, it's sheer fantasy."

"You think?" Millie was losing interest. "It's all very well speculating but there's no way we can get any proof, is there? Ooh, hang on, though—what about fingerprints? We could dust the sea horse!"

"D'you know, I think I forgot to pack my forensics kit," Tom said mockingly. "Anyway the thing's been mauled about since by Ray Grant when he brought it back here."

"So where does that leave us?" Like Millie, I badly wanted Zak around again, and getting to the truth was the only way to achieve that.

Tom shrugged. "Dunno. We could keep an eye on the suspects, maybe try breaking the alibis they've come up with."

It sounded vague and unsatisfying and I was itching to *do* something, take some kind of action.

"I bet I could do that." Millie was more amenable to his idea. "I'll go and have a chat with Corinne, throw in a few casual trick questions, that kind of thing."

"Yeah, of course you've got Corinne down as the most likely person to chuck a paperweight, haven't you?" Tom laughed, not seeming to take the situation very seriously at all.

"Yeah." Millie chuckled in return. "She's got the temperament *and* the motive—can't stand Tasha—and the best opportunity of anyone, being actually on the premises around the right time. I could practically snap the handcuffs on her right now."

"Stop fooling around." I was uptight. "You've already

said Corinne isn't stupid."

"In which case"—Millie was irrepressible—"I'll go for the next most probable. And that's you, I'm afraid, Tom."

"What?" He nearly fell off his chair.

"Absolutely. It was ages before you came into the house, you said so yourself, loads of time to grab the sea horse, ride over to the neighbors', and lob it through their window."

He put down the pen. "You're right so far but *why* would I try to get Tasha thrown out?"

"Not Tasha—her boyfriend." Millie giggled. "All you guys are jealous of Zak because he's better looking, a better rider, better—"

"You cheeky witch!" Tom lunged at her and she ran away shrieking, with him chasing her.

I felt annoyed at their childish behavior, which showed clearly they didn't feel anywhere near as concerned as I was about the problems the family at Beacon Lodge were having. As always I took myself off to talk things through with my real Best Friend. Jade was pleased to see me and listened properly, her sensitive ears pricked forward as I stroked her neck and told her the whole story.

"I need to do something positive, something physical," I said. She nudged me agreeably. "We've missed out on our picnic and there's not much point joining Val's cross-country lesson. Maybe we should take off and do some detective work on our own."

The thought was appealing, so before everyone arrived to tack up and prepare for Val's class I got my pony ready and rode her quietly down the drive to the main gate. Here I hesitated, not sure which direction to take. There was the cliff trail, but I couldn't imagine finding any clues there; and there was the ride to the cove, but that meant going through the Grants' land.

"I'm not sure that gate will be unlocked anyway," I told Jade. "Tom said Ray was furious about his smashed window so he's probably padlocked it shut to keep out Beacon Lodge riders."

If I was to be a detective, though, I figured I needed to inspect the scene of the crime, so eventually I turned my pony right and found the turn into the front entrance of the Grant house. Tom was right, it wasn't far, and I could also understand Corinne mistaking the turning for some kind of shortcut. There were no gates and not even a house name or number; it looked like just a gravel lane curving away between overhanging trees. Once I'd ridden quietly round the first bend it was quite a surprise to see how close we were to the front of the house. The gates were here, tall wrought-iron ones, firmly shut and flanked each side by a row of solid fencing. Short of ringing the bell and asking permission to enter it seemed impossible to get any nearer. Disappointed, I moved Jade onto the grassy verge.

"Oh well, it was a worth a try. Let's go back and have a rethink—" As I spoke I noticed that the shrubbery bordering the lane at this point was slightly flattened, the ground around it looking trodden and muddied. "Someone's been through there, look, Jade!"

She obligingly turned her head and pushed forward, following the line of bent branches and snapped twigs. After a few steps the vegetation thinned and I could no longer find any discernible trail, but I kept her walking between the closely packed trees. We were following the line of fence that presumably encircled the entire Grant property and—I stopped and peered closely. There was one panel jutting out slightly, almost as though it was loose. Jade stood completely still while I leaned out of the saddle and shook it experimentally.

"It moves!" Excited, I slid to the ground and moved the panel sideways, creating a gap big enough for us to ride through.

We were still under the shelter of trees, a narrow belt that bordered the formal, manicured gardens surrounding the Grants' house, where shuttered windows gave a blank, empty look. I hoped very much it *was* empty but was too fired up not to carry on now. Keeping well into the shadows, we moved forward till we reached the back of the house with me peering intently at every window frame.

"There it is!" I squeaked, pointing to where a sheet of ply had been fitted, obviously a temporary measure till the shattered glass could be replaced.

I debated whether to risk going closer to look for clues but decided against it—if I was seen now I could pretend

I'd merely gotten lost, but if they found me snooping around the house it would take a lot more explaining. It seemed the only thing I'd proved was that *anyone* could have smashed that window, and that fact wasn't any help at all! Thinking hard, I carried on riding, looking all around me for anything that might be a clue. We'd left the formal gardens behind, and from the salty tang of the air and distant murmur of lapping waves, I realized we were approaching the beach. I still intended doing a "little girl lost" act if Ray Grant spotted me, but when Jade's hooves touched the first strip of sand all my "detecting" ambitions were forgotten and we both became distracted by the powerful lure of the sea.

"We really ought to go back," I said reluctantly, but she pranced and whinnied eagerly, exhilarated by the tantalizing sight and smell of the beach. "Okay, maybe just a quick paddle."

We splashed joyfully through the shallows, sending clouds of glittering spray soaring around us.

"D'you know," I told her recklessly, "we're already so wet we might just as well go the whole way and have a swim!"

She plunged and snorted—Jade's equivalent of saying, "Yes, yes, YES!"—so I quickly stowed her saddle with my boots and jeans on a big dry rock. There was no hesitation at all. Jade walked swiftly, purposefully through the waves until the seabed shelved and dropped away and there we were, swimming in the cool, silky waters of the cove. It was, as ever, pure bliss, and the feeling of togetherness, a total emotional unity with Jade, was the strongest I'd ever experienced. I lay along her back, not so much riding as being transported through the ocean by a fabulous sea creature. Literally carried away by the sheer heady sensation, I didn't realize how far Jade's powerful swimming had taken us till I saw we were now alongside the towering height of Tiber Cliffs.

"We're not supposed to be this close." I pulled myself together in an attempt to be sensible. "Come on, Jade, we'd better turn back."

The swell diversified here, waves breaking and slapping against rocky outcrops or lapping gently within the sheltered pools they made, and my eye was suddenly caught by the sight of a boat almost hidden from view as it bobbed peacefully in one of these inlets.

"Look, Jade." I pointed to its name. "The *Sea Horse*. That's what you are too—oh!"

A dark, thin face appeared briefly from behind the boat, and I realized there must be a cave cut into the cliff behind it. I certainly wasn't in detective mode; in the excitement of our swim I'd almost forgotten what I was supposed to be doing, but my natural curiosity was aroused. Instead of turning Jade away to swim back along the cove, I guided her through the rocks into the pool. From here I could see inside the cave and was surprised to see two figures moving boxes around in its greenish light. Jade, swimming easily, snorted as we got nearer, and one of them looked up sharply.

"Jeez! Who's *that*?"

"Hiyah, Paul." I recognized him at once and waved cheerfully. "It's me, Caitlin."

"She knows you!" The other one stepped back out of sight. "*Do* something, quick!"

To my utter amazement Paul lunged forward, diving

into the water and quickly reaching us with a strong over-arm crawl. I didn't have time to speak or even to think before he reached up and grabbed me, yanking me off Jade's back and into the water. I still held the reins but he wrenched them out of my grasp as with a one-armed side-stroke he swam back toward the cave, dragging me with him. It was as rapid and as horribly unexpected as that. Within minutes I was shoved and hustled into the dank cave and could only watch in horror as Jade, frightened and disoriented without me, swam swiftly out of the sheltered pool.

Chapter Twelve

My reaction was based far more on fear for my pony than for myself. I let out a scream, kicked back hard against Paul's legs, and tried to break free. He swore loudly and clamped a hand over my mouth.

"What are you *doing*?" The other man sounded almost as shocked as me.

"You said I had to stop her," Paul snarled and swore again when I lashed out with my feet once more.

"I meant go over and spin her some sort of story—not kidnap her!" There was real fury in his voice. "What are you aiming to do with her now?"

"I don't know." Paul's hand was still covering my mouth. "Let me think. If her horse gets back to shore—

ow, she's biting me now!"

"And I'll do it again," I spat out. "What d'you mean *if* she gets back? I need to make sure she's safe, I'll call her—"

"You keep quiet or I'll chase her out in the ocean and drown her." He shook his bitten finger vengefully.

"But—"

"Shut up, I mean it!" He sounded as though he did so I closed my mouth immediately.

"Sit there." He shoved me roughly onto a wooden crate. "And don't say a word till I figure out what we can do."

The other man called him a few choice names and the two of them went into a huddle while I peered anxiously out of the cave, my heart pounding as I tried desperately to catch a glimpse of Jade. She'd be far away now, hopefully galloping up the beach and through Ray Grant's grounds. I wouldn't let myself consider the alternative—that she'd taken the wrong turn, swimming out of the cove, and was even now battling the waves and strong current of the open sea. She—I stopped and held my breath. I could just make out the break in the rocks, the entrance to the quiet pool where the *Sea Horse* still bobbed gently.

There, her head turning anxiously as she scoured the cliffs, was my own sea horse, Jade, not swimming away at all but patently, wonderfully looking for me. I risked a sidelong glance at the two men and, barely moving a muscle, gave the long, low whistle my pony knew so well. Paul's head shot up as he glared at me.

"What was that?"

I shook my head as if in despair, pretending to cry until he shrugged and returned to his muttered conversation. I didn't dare risk whistling again, but there was no need: Jade had heard me and was swimming strongly toward the cave, already passing the moored boat in the pool. Careful to maintain my posture of slumped defeat I waited till my pony was only yards away from the cave entrance, then with one mighty leap I dived into the water, reaching her with three panicky strokes.

"Go, Jade, go!" I wasn't riding, just clinging on, but she obeyed instantly, striking out across the inlet to reach the gap in the outcrop of rocks. I heard an oath and the sound of a splash behind us and knew Paul had dived in to catch me.

"You're much faster than he is," I whispered in my brave

pony's ear. "Just keep going, Jade, swim for your life!"

She felt more powerful than ever, carrying me swiftly across the calm waters of the pool, and I knew that even a strong swimmer like Paul wouldn't be able to match her speed. It was only when a motor roared into life behind us that I felt a stab of fear. He had swum straight to the *Sea Horse*, and when I glanced nervously over my shoulder the boat was already turning in pursuit. Jade kept going, swimming through the break in the rocks and heading straight for the shore of the cove. Paul, gunning the engine to full speed, was right behind us. I tightened my grip on Jade's mane, expecting at any minute to be plucked once again from her back. He was using a different tack this time, though, sweeping past us in a curving arc, then driving the *Sea Horse* straight at us. Trying not to scream, I touched Jade's sides and turned her away, changing direction so we were now heading seaward. The nightmare seemed to last forever: Four times we tried to get past the boat and four times he headed us grimly, pushing us farther and farther out into the deeper waters of the cove. I knew once he'd forced us beyond the sheltering arch of the cliffs Jade would be fighting against the colder, turbulent waves of the ocean, a battle too much for even a brave and magnificent horse like her.

I could feel her beginning to weaken and desperately I tried getting past the boat one more time. As we turned beachward to face the *Sea Horse* I saw a sight that made my terrified spirits soar. Two riders, their horses surging strongly through the waves, were heading toward us! Paul, his back to them, his senses concentrated on trying to force Jade out of the cove, didn't see them, and the engine noise from the *Sea Horse* was so loud he had no warning of their approach. I could see them clearly, though, and my heart banged against my rib cage as I recognized Zak and Tasha. Desperate to stop Paul turning and spotting them, I called out to him, my voice sounding frightened and shaky even to me.

"What d'you think you're going to achieve, Paul? Let us go, you can't do this!"

"Just watch me," he shouted grimly, keeping the boat steady in front of my bravely swimming pony to block any chance of our escape.

Behind him, Jet was now so close I could see the black horse's flaring nostrils as Zak brought him alongside the boat. Terrified and exhausted as I was, I still felt my heart leap exultantly as, with one strong, muscular leap, he swarmed onto the *Sea Horse*'s deck. Paul spun round but before he could move Zak was on him, his fist curled, his blue eyes gleaming. He looked—well, just *wonderful*. Trembling, I tried to smile at him, then flinched away as he raised his arm furiously at the snarling, swearing Paul. Tasha, her red hair streaming like a pennant, picked up Jet's reins with one hand and brought Sabrina close beside me.

"It's all right, Caitlin, you're safe now. Slide onto Jet and I'll lead Jade back. You're both completely spent."

It was true, I could barely summon the strength to slither from my rapidly weakening pony and slump against Jet's strong neck. Tasha soothed and comforted, helping Jade gently through the water until we all reached the shallows. I almost fell from the black horse, slithering awkwardly to stand beside Jade, my legs trembling, my arms wrapped around her while her sides heaved as she took in healing gulps of air.

"So, did Zak beat Paul up?" Millie's eyes sparkled at the thought. "I bet he was fantastic!"

"I didn't see, I was a bit busy getting back to shore," I said drily. "Paul had one heck of a black eye, apparently, but you'll have to ask Tasha for details."

"I wouldn't think she saw much either," Tom said. "From what you told us, she was more concerned with getting you and Jade back to shore."

"Yeah, she was great." I looked at them both. "So do you want the whole story or what? You didn't take the detective idea seriously, I know, but—"

"Yeah we did." Millie was indignant. "Just not quite as seriously as you, that's all. I mean, not everybody goes storming into a criminal's lair, do they! So come on, just what *were* Paul and his creepy mate doing out there in that cave?"

"His creepy mate is his brother and the police have him too. They've had a nice little sideline to their fishing expeditions," I explained. "It's called smuggling. Paul was very keen to keep people away from the cove and particularly Tiber Cliffs, where they used the cave for storing stuff. There were never any cliff falls, he made that up to keep swimmers away, but Ray Grant's closure of the track suited him much more. He was delighted and couldn't wait to start building that fence, knowing everyone except Beacon Lodge guests would be barred. "

"So he must have been even more thrilled when Tasha flung the sea horse paperweight through Ray's window," Millie said thoughtfully. "Did you find out how she did it?"

"She didn't," I said simply. "Paul did. He knew about the rows she kept causing and was pretty sure *she'd* get the blame if he used Ed's sea horse to do the damage. That meant Ray, who was itching for an excuse to keep out *all* riders, would refuse to let the Meadows family across his land anymore, giving Paul and his brother more opportunity for their smuggling game."

"But the access to the cove is all sorted too, isn't it?" Tom looked at me. "Val and Ed were so grateful to you, they explained all about it, didn't they?"

I nodded. "All those important meetings Val has been attending were to investigate Ray's claim on the strip of land leading to the beach. Tasha was right—his 'proof' was a clever forgery, and Val's been able to expose it."

"Phew," Tom whistled. "No wonder they didn't like Tasha's in-your-face methods. They were just going along with Ray's demands till they could prove him wrong legally."

"What, with a big court case and everything?" Millie pulled a face. "That'll take forever and I want to ride to the beach with Zak *now!*"

I laughed at her. "Don't worry, you selfish little cat. The fence is being demolished as we speak, and Ray Grant won't be bothering Beacon Lodge at all in the future."

Tom let out another long whistle. "You don't mean he's going to jail?"

"Val didn't want to press charges about the forgery— she's just grateful to be losing him as a neighbor. Ray Grant's greed makes him totally unscrupulous, just as Tasha said. He swindled her uncle out of cash and this business with the boundary was a blatant attempt to cheat

217

again, this time to get more money for his house."

"He's selling it?" Millie sounded surprised.

"Yeah, that's what it's all been about. He can ask far, far more for his house if he can claim it comes with exclusive rights to a private beach. We're talking mega money here."

"Right, I'm following you so far." Tom was frowning. "But how come he gave Beacon Lodge permission to ride across the bit of land he cheated to get?"

"To keep Val and Ed quiet until after he'd done the deal with the new buyer. Grant thought if he told the Meadows family he'd allow them access for their holiday business they wouldn't give him any trouble, and at least it would give him time to get the sale through. He couldn't care less that as soon as the new owners moved in they'd probably want to exclude everyone from their 'private beach.' Tasha told Zak that Beacon Lodge would soon be barred too, and she was right."

"Grant didn't know Val was working like mad to prove his claim was illegal," Tom said thoughtfully. "And presumably he also didn't know what those two brothers were up to out there on Tiber Cliffs. Paul should be locked up and the key thrown away for what he tried to do to you, Caitlin."

"He panicked. I don't think he ever intended to get *that* heavy," I said. "He's more your small-time, opportunist crook. I had a vague suspicion when I found the fence panel had been loosened. Paul was the most likely person to do that, wasn't he?"

"Hey, just a minute," Millie said suddenly. "It's all very well you becoming a Tasha fan because she was right all along and she helped rescue you, but what about that guilty look of hers you reckon you spotted?"

"That's what she and Zak were doing in the cove. Tasha confessed to him that although she hadn't smashed Ray's window she *had* flung the sea horse out the window in sheer temper when she went looking for Val. Zak's had suspicions about Paul before now and knew the guy could easily have seen the thing being hurled out. And that's exactly what happened. Paul saw Tasha go tearing into the house in a rage and was working right outside the window when she threw it. It only took him a few minutes to reach the Grant house, slip in through the panel he'd loosened, and do the damage."

"You have to admit Caitlin's first attempt at being a detective has been pretty spectacular!" Tom tugged my hair gently. "I bet the Meadows family are over the moon."

"They're pretty pleased," I admitted modestly. "I've got an open invitation to stay at Beacon Lodge anytime I like."

"Lucky old you!" Millie moaned. "Swimming with Zak every day—how brilliant would that be!"

"Swimming with Jade is my thing," I said firmly. "And Jade is the real hero of the story. I still can't believe the way she came back to find me!"

This was absolutely true and every time I think about our adventure at Beacon Lodge I shiver with amazement at how incredible my pony had been. Life is looking better and better for the two of us. Mum got the job and a move to somewhere lovely on the coast is all lined up so daily swimming could soon become a reality. It's going to take a while to get over my first-ever crush—I still think Zak is gorgeous and I often daydream about they way he looked when he came to my rescue—but I'm glad he's happy with Tasha, who, for all her fiery ways, loves him to bits in return. I'm going to stay in touch with my friends Millie and Tom too, and I expect there'll be loads of times when we talk about the extraordinary story of not one, but *three* sea horses.

OTHER BOOKS BY
JENNY HUGHES

JENNY HUGHES lives in Dorset, England. She has written twenty-two horse novels for young adults, which have been published in eight countries. Jenny's books are based on her experience working at a farm, at a riding school, and with polo ponies; but most of all they spring from her deep love of horses and the joy of sharing her life with such amazing beings.